A LONG-AGO
MURDER

JOHN A. RUSSO

Burning Bulb
PUBLISHING

A Long-Ago Murder
by **John A. Russo**

Burning Bulb Publishing
P.O. Box 4721
Bridgeport, WV 26330-4721
www.BurningBulbPublishing.com

Cover designed by Gary Lee Vincent.

First edition.

Paperback edition ISBN 978-1-964172-17-0

*This book is dedicated to all my friends
from Farnsworth Avenue.*

IN MEMORIAM

With rue my heart is laden
For golden friends I had
For many a rose-lipped maiden
And many a lightfoot lad.

By brooks too broad for leaping
The lightfoot lads are laid
The rose-lipped maids are sleeping
In fields where roses fade.

—Alfred Edward Housman
Shropshire Lad

CHAPTER 1

When we were both thirteen years old, my best friend, Ron Demick, was gruesomely mutilated and murdered. Three older boys were accused of doing it as part of a satanic ritual, and they were convicted and sent to prison, where they served twenty-eight years of their life sentences before finally being freed because a witness recanted vital testimony.

After a long career as a writer and filmmaker, I decided to try to solve that long-ago murder.

Back in 1967, I read a book about King Vidor's attempt to solve the 1922 murder of famous silent movie director Desmond Taylor. Mabel Normand and Mary Miles Minter, two of Taylor's beautiful, flamboyant starlets, became prime suspects. Rumors and suspicions ran rampant, but nothing was ever proven, and nobody was ever arrested.

I thought that if King Vidor, director of such classics as *Northwest Passage, War and Peace,* and *Duel in the Sun*, could try to solve a cold case, then so could I, even though my movies were low-budget horror flicks, not lavish spectacles like Desmond Taylor's. My horror film, *Intensive Scare*, spawned three sequels featuring a fictional serial killer, Wayne Calley, who raped and killed beautiful young women, then sliced off their ears and wore them as a necklace. I named him after actor John Wayne, who had disappointed me by becoming a cheerleader for the Vietnam War, and for Lieutenant William Calley, who had perpetrated the Mi Lai Massacre. I gave Wayne Calley a back story intended to make movie audiences reflect upon the evils of that war, but I think most of them only cared about the chills and thrills they got while eating their popcorn.

Be that as it may, my movies weren't just gore fests. They rippled with social and cultural conflicts and complex characters. I studied the investigative methods of policemen, private detectives, CSI investigators, medical examiners, and profilers. I conducted prison interviews with actual serial killers. I felt that if I hadn't chosen filmmaking, maybe I would have become a homicide detective or a prosecuting attorney. I started to believe that if I gave it a try, I could unravel the cold, cold case of my childhood.

One advantage would be my notoriety. My name is David Cristi, and I would be a door opener. Everybody in my small hometown knew about me and my movies. They didn't turn up their noses at the kind of movies I made. The fact that I made any movies was a big deal to them. I was sure that most people would be willing to talk to me if I told them I was laying the groundwork for a feature movie or an HBO documentary.

When King Vidor concluded his investigation, he believed that he had figured out who shot Desmond Taylor, but he never published his findings. A true-crime writer found them in a safety deposit box after Vidor's death and reconstructed the director's theories and surmises. Only then, years later, had the entire story been published. It could be that Vidor had thought that his conclusions were too dangerous or too embarrassing to the reputations of powerful people for him to risk coming forward with them.

I knew that what I was itching to do wasn't without danger. I understood if I unmasked the killer, he might be long dead. And if he wasn't dead, he might try at long last to kill *me* so he wouldn't ever have to face justice.

CHAPTER 2

Clairton, Pennsylvania, is the town I grew up in, only twelve miles from the heart of downtown Pittsburgh, and back then, it had a thriving population of about 25,000. The Clairton Works of United States Steel Corporation was the world's largest producer of coke for making steel, plus coke by-products such as naphthalene and toluene that likely contributed to the high rate of cancer, emphysema, and COPD in our vibrant little town, but we didn't think about that very much, if at all, when I was a kid.

I lived with my parents on Farnsworth Avenue, a three-block-long maple-lined street of four-room wooden duplexes built by the steel company in the 1930s to house the large influx of laborers who soon rushed in to fill them. In 1933, soon after they were married, my parents, Angeline and Johnny, took out what was, at the time, an intimidating mortgage of $3,000 for half a duplex in the middle of the avenue.

I was born two months premature on September 2, 1939, and was not expected to live. I had no eyebrows or fingernails and only weighed four pounds. I had to be put immediately into an incubator in the maternity ward, and after I was brought home from the hospital, I was kept in a wicker basket with a bright light bulb shining down on me to keep my blood circulating and my lips from turning blue.

That September, Adolf Hitler invaded Poland and launched World War Two. Much later in life, after becoming a film enthusiast, I discovered that 1939 was a banner year for fabulous movies: *Gunga Din, State Fair, The Wizard of Oz,* and *Gone with the Wind.* I still wonder how the world could produce such great art while gearing up for genocide and mass murder. There were a hundred million people dead when it was all over.

I have vivid memories of ration stamps and black-out curtains. I remember how people on our street ran outside to spot airplanes each time they heard one flying over, in case it was Japanese or German. I remember the day our next-door neighbor, Grace Demick, pounded on our front door, gleefully crying out to my mother, "Angie! *Angie!* Hitler is *dead!*" My mother became just as gleeful as Grace was, and they danced and laughed in our living room as they turned on the radio to catch more news about Hitler's death. I asked them why they were so happy that someone had died, and they hugged and kissed me and told me that Adolf Hitler was one of the evilest people in the whole world, and now that he was dead, the war might soon be over. They said it would be nice if Tojo and Hirohito would commit hara-kiri. I asked what that was, and they wouldn't tell me.

My dad celebrated Hitler's death after his work shift was over that day, and he came home in a drunken rage and beat my mother up, splitting her lip and chipping one of her front teeth. I tried to pull him away from her, but he was unmoved by my tears and smacked me aside. I ran down to the basement and curled up on the cold concrete floor, shivering and crying and

hoping he wouldn't kill her. I lived in terror all my childhood, but I was never a kid who dove under the theater seats during scary scenes in the Frankenstein and Dracula movies. Some friends did that, but I could always tell myself, "It's only a movie." Maybe that was because the absolute terror was inside my own home. My father was a brutal alcoholic, a Jekyll and Hyde. My mother and I lived in constant fear of his

10

violent mood swings. Even when he was being his warm and fuzzy version of himself, we had to remain wary. If we grumbled at how scared of him we were, he wouldn't repent and change his ways; he would only get mad and then madder. He could flip at any moment.

One of the worst incidents happened on my sixth birthday, which fell on Labor Day that year. There was a steel workers' picnic at an amusement park called Kennywood, famous for its pony rides, penny arcade, Ferris wheel, and roller coasters. Our school picnics were always held there in the spring, but I had yet to experience one because I was now entering first grade, and my first school picnic was still nine months away. It was a hot, sunny Saturday, and groups of steel workers, including my father, were getting drunk and having a raucously good time. My mother took me to Kiddy Land, the park section with rides for little children. Now, we were watching an egg-throwing contest, and I had never seen one and was astounded by its messiness. Grown men were pelting each other with raw eggs, the yolks splattering all over their arms, faces, and clothes. My dad was a neatness fanatic and stayed well back from the action and pushed me and my mom back from it, too.

My parents started fighting right after we got home, a pattern that was to be repeated dozens of times more as I grew older and a thing that had already happened many times previously. But this fight was more vicious and terrifying than some of the others. My father punched one of my mother's eyes shut, gashed her cheek, and twisted her arm behind her back while I cried and screamed and begged him to stop. I tried to shield my mother from him, but she grabbed some clothesline and ran down the cellar stairs, saying that she would hang herself. I ran down the stairs after her, trying to pull the rope out of her hands before she could tie it over the I-beam. I clung to her, said I loved her, and desperately, helplessly promised that when I grew up, I'd take care of her. What I did not realize till I got older was that she was as neurotic as my father, but in different ways, and for many years, she would use that promise I made as a helpless child to manipulate me.

All through my childhood and into my teen years and beyond, when my father would beat my mother, she would try to call the cops on him, but he would stop her by ripping the phone out of the wall. One day, she came at him with a butcher knife, but she was a tiny woman, no match for his enraged strength, so he easily wrenched the knife out of her hand and kept on slapping and punching her. There were other times when she managed to run next door and use Grace Demick's phone; then the cops would arrive with sirens wailing. They'd handcuff my father and take him to jail, and we'd have three days of sad, bitter peace.

One of the worst of times was when my mother would run away from home and not take me with her, and I wouldn't see her for several weeks, not knowing if she was alive or dead. My father would then be sugary sweet to me and cook suppers and pack lovely lunches and give me his loose change and make me tell him what a "good daddy" he was. If I asked about my mother, he'd say, "Don't worry, son, she'll be back." But I always thought she may have killed herself. I'd cling to the hope that she might be staying at her sister's house in Pittsburgh, but I had no way of knowing that, and I couldn't phone her, and she didn't phone me because our phone had been ripped out of the wall. Then she'd finally come back, and I'd be overwhelmed with relief, and my father would treat me and my mother much better for a while, till the next binge and the next fight.

When I was in the first grade, I thought I was the only kid in the room who didn't have a family as sweet and loving as the one in my *Dick and Jane* reader. My dad didn't take me sledding or help me make a birdhouse like the dad in the book did. My dad terrorized me in real life and my nightmares. In grade school, I would get vicious headaches that started at the back of my neck and stretched over the top of my skull and into my forehead. At the time, I didn't know that they were probably migraines caused by extreme duress.

Despite all that, I always got excellent grades in school and made the Honor Roll. I was scared not to because of my angry father and my stern mother, who was basically a good, unselfish, long-suffering person who could also be demanding and domineering. I dreaded coming home from school daily because I feared what I might find. I'd tiptoe through the small house, from the basement to the two upstairs bedrooms, hoping I didn't see my mom hanging in a closet or from the I-beam in the cellar or that I didn't find my mom and dad both dead with butcher knives sticking out of their bodies.

My father would usually ruin every holiday, especially Christmas, because so much booze was flowing at all the bars in town from Christmas to New Year's. He would come home and fly into a drunken rage every time he had to put the tree up, probably because he hated any task that interfered with his celebrating. He'd curse my mother for not buying a tree with a small enough trunk to fit easily into the stand or for not buying the long-needled kind that didn't shed so many needles all over the carpet. He'd work himself into a fit and yell at her and beat her up, and then sometimes the cops would come, and he'd land in jail again, and my mother would often leave again and not tell me where she was going. And so, once again, I'd spend the holidays in utter dread over what she may have done to herself.

When I was about in the fifth grade and had learned how to use a hammer and nails, I'd go to a lot behind a confectionary store where Christmas trees were sold, and I'd gather up fallen branches before they could turn brown, then take them home and make my own "tree" by nailing them to a four-foot-long

13

two-by-two. I'd make paper decorations or scavenge broken ones from people's trash and hang them on my homemade tree. Then I'd spread a white cloth underneath and place my toy cars on it. It was a way of having my own Christmas tree alone, without any vicious fights around it. As a kid, I wasn't aware of the pathos in this, but later, as an adult, I became aware of it, and it saddens me when I look back on it.

Almost all the men on Farnsworth Avenue worked in the mills and were happy that they could provide a good living for their families. In those days, on a millworker's salary, their kids could go to college. Or they could choose to work on a production line, like their fathers did, and still earn an excellent wage and take pride in their lives. Most women did not take jobs but stayed home and cared for the kids and the housework. I never heard any of them complain about this. I'm not making any social statement against it; I'm just saying that's how it was.

The women who had decent husbands and unthreatening marriages seemed reasonably happy. On the other hand, when a woman and her children were tied to an abusive husband, there was almost no way out financially. Those women mostly stayed and took their beatings, like my mother did. So did Grace Demick, the woman next door, whom I very much liked. Her

husband, Tillman, was an alcoholic but not an abusive one. Once, he told my dad, "We're both drunks, Johnny, but I admit it, and you don't." My dad turned red and clenched his fists, but he refrained from punching Tilly, his drinking buddy.

Up until I was around age eighteen, I believed strongly in the Catholic religion, and it was hard for me to understand how people could profess to love one another and swear to do God's will and yet destroy each other's lives due to inner demons that they were utterly unable to acknowledge, much less conquer.

14

Because my father was, in essence, a split personality, with the two sides of him constantly warring with each other, one side of him showed me the wrong way to be, while the flip side showed me how nice it would be if we all treated each other with dignity and respect. When he was what he called a "good daddy," he was one of the most admirable men you'd ever want to meet. But when his lousy side took over, he was evil incarnate.

He had many innate talents that he had failed to cultivate, which was his primary source of frustration and hateful rage against his job and the world. He was handsome and quite vain about it, to the point where he always came home from work showered, shampooed, and wore a clean white shirt and crisply ironed slacks. When he was sixteen, a program manager heard him singing in a bar one day for nickels and dimes and offered him a spot on the radio, which was a big deal in those days. But *his* father, who was probably even meaner than he was, had made him drop out of school and start working in a coal mine at age fourteen, and he beat him with a strap when he said he wanted to be a singer. Then came the Great Depression, which put the final nail in the coffin of my father's dreams. He became a bitter alcoholic who took it out on me and my mother.

His example taught me that I had to follow my dreams and not settle for less. I eventually yearned to become a writer after I got my first clue that I had some talent in that direction, and I became determined to give it my best shot. I told myself that even if I failed, I would not have to gaze bitterly at my face in the mirror for the rest of my life and wonder what would have happened if only I had tried. In other words, I didn't want to be like my father.

CHAPTER 3

Ronald Demick and I were the same age and were best friends all through grade school and partly through junior high school, up until he was murdered along with two other boys.

Ron was the only son of our next-door neighbors, Tillman and Grace Demick. He and I got into things that our other friends weren't interested in or made fun of us for, like taking and then developing our photos or creating our own crystal set radios. We did These unique things apart from others, but we played sandlot baseball with all the other kids. Since about twenty kids around us grew up on Farnsworth Avenue, we almost always had enough to form two pick-up teams.

We were fierce about our addiction to baseball, and we all wanted to be "top picks" among our friends and worked hard at it. Almost every day in the summer, we'd walk about a mile up to Keenan Field, play baseball till noon, go home and eat lunch, then go to the Clairton swimming pool. We'd come home for dinner, and after that, we'd walk back up to Keenan Field to play baseball some more till it got too dark to see the ball.

One day, when Ron and I were walking from the sandlot up the alley to our duplex, we were set upon by some older kids from another street. Their leader was a no-good ruffian named Biff Conley, and everybody our age feared him and his gang. There were five of them, bigger and stronger than we were, and they punched us and clipped our legs out from under us, then pulled our sneakers off, tied the laces together, and tossed our shoes toward the telephone pole wires as many times as it took till they were left dangling where we could never reach them. The bullies laughed like hell. Then two of them straddled each of us, grinding our bodies into the hard black cinders, while two others pulled our T-shirts up, and Biff Conley said, "We're givin' you two punks a pink belly!" He slapped our naked stomachs till they turned red. We squirmed and hollered, but he wouldn't let up. It was not only painful but terrifying to us because we had heard that in giving a Pink Belly to a younger kid from another street, Biff and his buddies had ruptured that kid's appendix, and he had almost died.

When they were done having fun, they let Ron and me get up and limp home, our stomachs red and sore and our stocking feet hurting from the jagged cinders in the alley. Tilly bought Ron a new pair of sneakers without punishing him, but my dad yelled at me and gave me a whipping. I wailed, "Daddy...daddy...please...I'll use a clothesline pole and knock my shoes down from the wires!"

"Go ahead and electrocute yourself!" he shouted.

That scared me enough that I clammed up and took my punishment.

My mother hung back and didn't say a word because we both knew that if she spoke up, he'd turn on her. He made me describe the older kids as best I could, and I gave him Biff Conley's name and said he was the only one I knew. He stormed out of the house and went looking for them, and when he came home, his knuckles were skinned, and he smelled of whisky. He washed his hands in the kitchen sink, and my mother meekly got him a couple of Band-Aids. We were both scared because he kept an iron pipe under the front seat of his car, and he might have done something that would get him put in jail for a long time. We couldn't survive without his paycheck. A day or two later, he made my mother use some of the household money he doled out to her to buy me a new but much cheaper and flimsier pair of sneakers from the five-and-ten-cent store.

Wearing our new shoes, Ron Demick and I were headed into the playground when we caught sight of Biff and his buddies through the chain-link fence. They spotted us, and we turned and ran, but they caught up to us. One was limping, two had scrapes and bruises, and Biff had a black eye. They slapped and punched Ron and judo-chopped him, but they didn't take our new shoes and fling them up onto the telephone pole wires.

They gave Ron slaps, punches, and kicks till they got tired of doing it, but they didn't do anything to me except swear at me and threaten me. Maybe it was because they were in fear of my father. In any case, they continued to leave me alone, but they picked on Ron every time they ran into him, all the way up until the week that Ron was murdered.

There were two other boys found murdered around the same time that Ron was, and all three bodies were found naked and mutilated, submerged in a pond not too far from a shack we had built in the woods. The first suspects that came to my mind were Biff Conley and his gang of bullies, and many people in Clairton who had had run-ins with them immediately began thinking along those same lines.

CHAPTER 4

When I was a kid, I woke up every day with ideas bubbling through my head, a trait that has served me well as a writer and filmmaker. Even now, at an advanced age, I still have a lot of energy, fresh ideas, and a haste to get started on them.

When I was in fourth grade and read *The Adventures of Tom Sawyer* and *The Adventures of Huckleberry Finn*, I got all fired up with the notion of digging a pirate cave in the hillside of our backyard. I was so fired up that I didn't even think about how badly my dad would beat me if I even turned over a single lump of sod.

I had already learned excitedly that we had a river, the Monongahela, somewhere on the other side of the woods behind our street. Even though I didn't know how far away it was or how to get there, I was pumped up with visions of being able to float on a raft someday, just like Huck, Tom, and Jim. In the meantime, having my pirate cave to play in seemed like a great thing and closer to hand. I couldn't wait to enlist Ron Demick and some other kids to help me dig, just like Tom got others to whitewash his Aunt Polly's fence. My imagination was so persistent that it often carried other kids along with it. When we all saw the Dracula and Frankenstein movies, I made dummies of the two famous movie monsters and two cardboard coffins for them. I got a bunch of my pals to help me dig graves at the edge of our baseball sandlot, and we buried the dummies in hopes that they would soon arise as the movie monsters did, which, of course, did not happen.

I saw the pirate cave idea as something based more on realistic anticipations. But it turned out to be one more of my early lessons on how difficult it could be to match dreams with reality. Five or six of us met up with our toy shovels in our backyard, but when we tried to get to work, we immediately found out that our pitiful little tools couldn't make a dent in the sod, and we had to give up. Probably a good thing because at least I didn't get my ass beaten.

I was always a dreamer and a would-be adventurer, not very content with doing ordinary things. Besides being unable to dig a pirate cave, one of my other early frustrations was that I was not allowed to read the story about knights and dragons at the back of my reader at school. The stories in the front of the book were read out loud in class by us kids, taking turns reading a paragraph at a time, and a lot of my classmates were such slow readers that we never got farther than halfway through the book. If I had gotten caught sneaking ahead to the knights and dragons' story, the teacher, Miss Forbes, a tall, bony, angular spinster with stiff, greasy black hair, would have beaten me with the big wooden paddle that she kept in the chalk trough.

Miller Avenue School had teachers who were so strict and mean that they would be considered child abusers by today's standards. Almost none of them were ever married, and even though what I'm about to say is a politically incorrect statement, I must say that they were perfect examples of what we call Old Maids. When I got old enough to know about the causes and effects of sexual frustration, I thought they must have all been suffering from it, and so they took it out on us. They all had paddles in their chalk troughs and used them at whim. We were forbidden to whisper to each other in class. I once got beaten repeatedly across my chest for merely turning my head slightly to one side, even though I didn't whisper across the aisle, which was a big no-no. All the paddles had holes drilled in them to create welts. All the desks were bolted to the floor so they wouldn't slide around and cause "discipline problems."

I was not too fond of that school. It was oppressive, scary, and boring because I was such a quick learner. I had to sit and wait while other kids struggled with their multiplication tables, standing in line and taking turns trying to recite them.

None of us got bullied in school because the bullies were stifled as much as everyone else while inside the building. But outside of school, it was a different story. All the steel towns in the Monongahela Valley were rough and tough. Fist fights were incited and looked forward to as a welcome spectacle. Bullying was rampant. I had my first fistfight when I was five years old with Ralph Gaston, who was one of the most challenging kids on Farnsworth. My mother caught us slinging our fists right in front of our house and beat my little behind with a slat from an orange crate.

I daydreamed a lot in the classroom but still got high grades because it was so easy for me. The mean teachers couldn't police my thoughts, so I dreamed a lot about the weekend battles we had started to have with a gang of kids around my age who lived on a street that bordered our sandlot. I don't remember how the ritual began, or even if I might have been the one who set it in motion, but it took place almost every Saturday in the fall if there wasn't rain. We fought each other with clubs, spears, and rocks, using garbage-can lids for shields. This sounds ridiculous to me now, but back then, I loved it. In my young imagination, we were knights going to war, something like the knights I never got to read about in the back of my fourth-grade reader.

These knightly "wars" were staged only in the fall because our spears and clubs were only pithy reeds of various thicknesses, and they only lost their greenness and softness when summer was over. We pulled them out of the ground

21

after their leaves had withered, the stalks had become hard, like wood, and they had dirt and stones clinging to their roots. The tall, thinner ones became spears, and the short, fat ones became clubs. The Farnsworth "troops" would charge at the opposing "troops," and both "armies" would let fly with the clubs, spears, and rocks. If you got hit with one of those short fat clubs full of clumped dirt and stones, it would hit you so hard it would knock you down. If your garbage can shield didn't stop all the rocks, you could have a bloody head.

We, Farnsworth Avenue kids, did a lot of dangerous things when we were away from the eyes of our parents. For a long time, we all had bows and arrows. I was once shot in the neck with an arrow from another boy's bow, and I pulled it out, and one of my friends threw up. We didn't want our parents to take away our bows, so we made up a story that a strange kid had hit me with a piece of broken glass at the playground. Because the wound was round and deep, not jagged, it was a transparent lie, but somehow, we got away with it.

We used to swim in the river, and back in those days, it was ugly, dark brown, and polluted. Fat human stools would sometimes float by while we were swimming. Five or six of my classmates were drowned in the Monongahela River. If anyone sunk beneath the surface, the water was so dark and murky that no one could see them to pull them out. Several young men, much older than I then, were objects of deep envy when they built their own raft, and I had to watch them dive off it and swim, wishing I could do that. I shuddered and had nightmares when I found out that three of them had drowned in that dark, black river.

We also used to play with gunpowder and blasting caps. Two kids were disfigured for life when they tossed a match into a big jar of black powder, and it exploded and engulfed them in flames. They were lucky to survive, but their faces

22

looked like melted wax after that, and no amount of plastic surgery could fix them.

An older boy was blinded when a blasting cap he was fooling with exploded in his face.

We used to steal the blasting caps from construction sites, and it's a wonder we could have managed to get our hands on actual dynamite. The sticks of dynamite had hollow places for the blasting caps to be inserted when the explosives were placed to take down a hillside. For some reason, the construction crews were sometimes careless with the blasting caps, maybe because they were less potent than the dynamite, but they were still exceedingly dangerous.

As kids, we were naive and foolish enough to use blasting caps in our "war games" in the woods, where we had built a shack and made swings by stealing bull ropes from the barges on the river and hanging them from huge tree limbs overhanging a creek. About ten kids from our street broke their arms or legs one summer from falling off the swings into the dry, rocky bed of the creek. Ron Demick was one of the ones who broke an arm about three weeks before he was murdered.

Clairton and the other steel towns in the Monongahela Valley were challenging, roughneck places where you had to be willing to fight, or else you'd be bullied, made fun of, and pushed around almost every day of your life. My father was my own personal bully, so I didn't need that role to be filled by other kids. But the crazy, dangerous things I did with the Farnsworth Avenue gang in my growing-up years made me streetwise and not willing to take anybody's guff. The daredevil stuff and the fist-fighting made me a good director of action sequences and cinematic brawls when I started directing movies.

CHAPTER 5

Clairton Junior-Senior High was a welcome respite from the stiflingly oppressive Miller Avenue Grade School. I transitioned in 1951 at age 12 and was placed into a college prep class encompassing what the administration considered the brightest students. I didn't realize this distinction at the time, which was based purely on IQ scores, and I was frustrated at being unable to be in the class that held most of my friends from Farnsworth Avenue. It was especially galling that Ron Demick wasn't in my class, and I didn't know why. As bright as I knew him to be, he must not have scored high enough on the IQ tests.

The stately three-story stone building took up a city block and was crammed with over 3,000 students, hundreds from the upscale communities of Baldwin and Pleasant Hills, relatively younger towns still needing their high schools. At this time, Clairton High was one of the top high schools in the country, so much so that you could get into most small colleges if you graduated in the upper third of your class.

We lived in a thriving little town, and we took it for granted and didn't appreciate it because we were born into it, and almost all of us had never lived anywhere else. We had three movie theaters that changed pictures twice a week, three bowling alleys, a rural city park with rustic shelters and a vast swimming pool with diving boards, several car dealerships, a couple of recreation halls, and playgrounds with softball fields. The shopping district had ice cream parlors and attractive stores of many kinds, and you could buy almost anything you needed without leaving town. If you couldn't find it in Clairton, you went across the river to McKeesport, twice as large at about 50,000 residents, and if you couldn't get it there, you went to Pittsburgh, which most people thought to be a pretty far trip back then -- and a little scary with its tall buildings.

I had highly motivated teachers who inspired me in many ways. They were dedicated to doing their best for the students, despite being paid little. Steelworkers got paid twice as much as teachers did. There were no teachers' unions. Many of my teachers supplemented their meager incomes by working each summer as painters and window washers in the schools for minimum wage.

My favorite teacher was my seventh-grade English teacher, Mr. Brevko. He was only 22 years old, a brand-new faculty member, and freshly graduated from a teachers' college. He had a beautiful young wife and a one-year-old baby girl. The main reason I liked him so much was that he often strayed from our English lessons and gave us pep talks that flattered us and made us feel good. His enthusiastic praise was designed to motivate us and bolster our egos, and I loved hearing it at that impressionable time of my life. "You're not children anymore," he would say. "You're young adults. You're ready to have adult experiences.

Some of you are more than ready. You may have already had some experiences that you're not telling your parents about, and there's not necessarily anything wrong with that because you're not far from adulthood. Adults are allowed to have private lives."

He would describe all the wonderful adult things beyond our horizons and about to happen to us. Every time I entered his classroom, I hoped to hear one of those special kinds of pep talks again. He had dark, wavy hair, a smooth, youthful face, and keenly alert brown eyes, and he was always so poised and

25

scholarly and self-confident that it was just how I hoped I would be a few years hence. His English class was my first class each weekday morning, and I could barely wait to take my seat.

But one day, he didn't show up for a week, and we had a substitute teacher with none of the charm and grace Mr. Brevko had. I found her so dull compared to him that I couldn't abide her and didn't even want to try. We were never told why he wasn't there, and I was disappointed every day as his absences continued. Somebody in my math class asked, "What's going on with Mr. Brevko?" And my math teacher said, "I can't say what it is yet."

My father said at the supper table that Saturday, "Why didn't you tell me your English teacher got arrested?"

My mouth felt open. Utterly stunned, I waited for my dad to laugh at his little joke, but instead, he said, "Don't tell *me* you didn't know."

I was speechless, so I just shook my head.

"That little pansy has been taking nude pictures of some of the girls in his classes," My father said. "Boys, too, the sickening pervert. He was arrested, but he's out on bail. There've been articles about it in the paper, but they don't print the young girls' names. But some of them already told on the little fart, and he's going to plead guilty."

I ran up to my room, threw myself down on my bed, and couldn't stop crying. The sobs were so violent they hurt my chest, and my pillow got soaked with tears.

My mother crept into my room and put her hand on my shoulder, but I snapped at her, "Leave me alone!"

Immediately after that, I realized I had treated her like my father would have. But it was too late to apologize. She had gone back downstairs.

Throughout the rest of my year in seventh grade, I had difficulty pushing aside my gullible enthrallment with Mr.

26

Brevko, which ended with the shock of finding out what kind of person he was. It wasn't until years later, when I was studying criminal behavior and writing screenplays and novels about sick-minded rapists and killers that I came to realize that his artfully constructed digressions in English class were discreetly disguised seductions. In our innocence, he told us we were virtual adults, ready for adult experiences. Our sweet, clever Mr. Brevko was grooming us to accept further advances from him when he should he find an opportunity to exploit some of us sexually.

Back in those days, over sixty years ago, we youngsters were shielded from the details of whatever he had done to some of the boys and girls from our school. The abused ones must have returned to classes because nobody seemed to be missing from school, and we could only guess which ones of us had been victimized by Mr. Brevko because, as far as I ever knew, none of them had admitted it to us students, only to their parents or the police.

A few weeks later, as my mom was putting supper on the table, my dad said, "Guess what, David? Your English teacher flew the coop. His wife says she doesn't know where he is. Maybe she's lying, maybe not. She told the cops she's divorcing him and moving far away from here; I don't know where, and she's taking their little girl with her."

I was dumbstruck. Every scrap of information that came my way, by hook or crook, just devastated and shattered my previous hero worship of Mr. Brevko.

For a long time, I never heard anything further about him. Adults kept mum. In those days, sex scandals weren't bandied about like they are now; such topics were taboo for the ears of children. My once revered English teacher disappeared, maybe into prison somewhere, but I couldn't find out. There was no Internet and no Google in those days. But he came sneaking back into my thoughts decades later when I was hit with a startling revelation about him that got me thinking about doing my investigation into Ron Demick's murder. Not just Ron's either because two other boys were killed along with Ron.

CHAPTER 6

As I worked my way through the eighth grade, I achieved a level of normalcy so far as school was concerned. My gang on Farnsworth Avenue was becoming less enthused about baseball, and we slowly weaned ourselves away from our pickup games because we were all becoming more interested in girls. The school was a refuge from my parents' terrifying fights, but I wouldn't say I liked it anyway.

I was still in the college prep class, and Ron Demick wasn't. But I became buddies with a boy named Mickey Jenkins, who wasn't in college prep either, but he was in one of my study periods. He was big and chubby, with a face full of freckles and a shock of unruly red hair, and he wasn't in with any of the "cool kids." However, he and I shared an interest in model airplanes and rocketry. Both of us had read a library book about Dr. Paul Goddard, who was called "the father of American rocket science." He was a voice crying in the wilderness about how our government needed to put vast amounts of money into building rockets to deliver bombs in case another world war should happen. As the only way to possibly put human beings on another planet. Mickey and I were extremely excited about this. During study periods, we would sit together. On our yellow tablets, we would draw pictures of rockets we might build together according to our unworkable designs -- except we didn't know enough to realize they wouldn't work.

We often got together after school and made our gunpowder, packing it into cardboard tubes with fuses and using the sandlot as our "laboratory." However, our homemade rockets got at most five feet into the air. Most of them just fell over, flamed, and sputtered bumpily over the sand, zigzagging all over the place until the gunpowder burnt up.

We had better luck with our little u-control airplanes. At least Mickey did. His plane was precisely assembled, primed, sanded, and painted according to the box's instructions, but I lacked his patience. I couldn't wait for the primer or the paint to dry, and I didn't do enough sanding so that the paint would blister; then I'd try to sand it down, and repeatedly, I painted over rough spots till finally, I quit. And when I tried to fly the thing, it was so heavy with bad coats of paint that it just bumped along and never got off the ground.

Despite all that, Mickey and I had fantasies of starting a model airplane club with me as president and him as secretary-treasurer. We knew that the Clairton American Legion Post had quite a few rooms on their second floor that were never used for anything, so we got bold enough to go in and ask to speak with an officer. When the bartender told us he was the sergeant-at-arms, we asked him if we could use one of the upper rooms as a weekly meeting place for our club. To our great surprise, even though he laughed at us, he readily gave us his permission.

We chose one of the rooms with great joy and made a sign for the door out of cardboard and crayons. We also brought a card table and chairs that Mickey's mother let us use. We decorated the walls with photos of airplanes torn from magazines.

While we were bringing some of the stuff in one day, a bunch of the American Legion members were storming and raging over vandalism that had occurred above Clairton Park, on Memorial Hill, and at one of the Catholic cemeteries in the central part of town. We tuned in to the bluster and anger and heard from the angry men that tombstones had been overturned in the cemetery and brass markers had been stolen from Memorial Hill. The costly markers had been placed there to honor soldiers from Clairton who had died in our various wars, and each one had a soldier's name on it. Little flags were placed near each plaque, and a service was held there each Memorial Day, which was sponsored by the American Legion.

We all knew why the brass markers were stolen without discussing it. Local junkyards were buying brass and copper for forty-seven cents a pound, which was quite a high price then, so people were collecting and selling it. They would even burn the insulation off copper extension cords, even if they had to steal the extension cords that people had strung out for their Christmas lights. When they had a good-sized hoard, they would take it to a junkyard.

Some of us kids shinnied up telephone poles and stole the grounding cables by cutting sections of them off with a hacksaw. These cables were about a half-inch thick and eight or ten feet long, representing quite a haul. But the electric company got wise and started making them of copper-plated steel instead of pure copper, easily detected as phony as soon as the junk man ran a magnet over it.

The brass markers from Memorial Hill were genuine brass, and nobody would question that. Whoever had stolen them was going to make a fortune. Or so it seemed. Until Biff Conley and two of his buddies, the same bullies who had given Ron Demick and me those very sore Pink Bellies were ratted out by one of the junkyard dealers. In short order, they were arrested and arraigned. But they were soon out on the streets again, acting sneeringly tough and smug. I figured they must have posted bail, maybe from ill-gotten gains they already had in their pockets, because even before they raided Memorial Hill, they had been beating up younger kids and confiscating their little collections of brass and copper. Many little collections could add up to a big score at forty-seven cents a pound. And brass plaques for a hundred and sixty soldiers killed in combat, at roughly ten pounds per plaque times at least forty-seven cents each, would tally about eight hundred dollars, to me a princely sum at that time, and nothing to scoff at for most Clairton mill workers either.

A couple of days before we knew that Biff Jenkins and his cronies had been sprung by their lawyer, Ron Demick and I had the misfortune of running into them at the playground. In their anger at having been caught for the Memorial Hill thefts, they were pushing younger kids off the swings and monkey bars and taking them over even though they were too big for them. Then, right in front of the playground teacher, they made four kids get up from a card table, sit down, and take over their game of Pinochle.

When they spotted Ron and me, they tossed the cards into a messy pile and came at us. Before we could do anything, they clipped us both down to the ground and started kicking us. Ron pleaded, "I have a broken arm! Let me be!" He held up his cast in plain sight, and it was already coated with yellow dirt, along with all the names of his classmates, signed crudely in ink. They just laughed at him and kicked him some more. But when the playground teacher screamed that she was calling the cops, they ran out through the gated chain-link fence and down a side street. It was clear that they didn't want to risk another arrest while they were out on bail.

But my bad luck run-ins with them weren't over. Not by a long shot.

The very next day, Mickey Jenkins and I walked up the hill after hanging some new posters in our little upstairs room at the American Legion. We passed up the playground rather than taking a chance that Biff Conley and his boys were in there. We decided to hang out in the woods behind Farnsworth Avenue, where my pals and I had built our little log shack.

32

To get down to the shack and the bull ropes hanging from the big tree, we headed into the alley behind the street, then past a confectionary store at one end of the alley and through what we called "the orchard" that was behind the store and consisted only of four or five peach trees. That's where we always went into the deep woods. At that time of year, April, it wasn't so hot and sweaty in the woods, and there weren't too many spiders and mosquitoes anxious to bite us as we worked our way down the dirt trail toward the clearing where the shack and the swings were.

Mickey and I dressed in the way typical of all Clairton boys at that time: jeans, sneakers, and T-shirts, mostly of solid colors without logos or cartoons. My T-shirt was red, and Mickey's was striped, red, yellow, and black that day.

We froze when we got close to the shack because we heard noises and knew that Biff Conley might be there. He had built the shack's roof for us -- well, not so much "built it" but stole it -- because he wanted our shack for his use. "I ain't gonna kick you little guys out. I wanna bring my girlfriend in here now and then, if you know what I mean," he told us with a sly wink. So, he and his cronies stole two double garage doors behind the sporting goods store owned by Mr. Harpster, waiting to be installed in a newly built garage. While we stood in awe and watched them, they made the floor of our shack out of one of those doors and the roof out of the other, and they covered the roof with tarpaper, and the floor with an old carpet somebody had put out to be taken away by garbage collectors. Mr. Harpster had immediately suspected Biff of stealing his garage doors and came down to our shack looking for them. he was standing on top of one of them and underneath the other without realizing it. We all thought that was hilarious.

Younger boys, including me, were forbidden to go near our shack whenever Biff or any of his gang were there, and I had clued Mickey in on that, so we were both rooted in our tracks.

33

Biff came out, pulling his pants up and buckling them. "Well, well, well," he said. "What we got here, a couple fucking Peeping Toms?"

Mickey and I stayed frozen, not knowing whether to run away or beg for forgiveness.

"Couple Peeping Toms in the making!" Biff said. Then he turned halfway around and yelled, "Hey, Mary Ann, get out here! With your clothes *off!*"

A muffled female voice came back at him. "Wait'll I put my shoes on!"

We heard some scuffling from inside the shack, and then a vastly overweight girl with greasy hair and pimples shuffled out. She looked about fourteen years old.

Mickey and I gawked at her, and finally, we took a couple of steps back. Biff Conley guffawed at us, and Mary Ann giggled.

"I can tell you two little kids ain't never seen a naked woman before," Biff said. "Take a good look, but you ain't gettin' none. But at least you'll be able to jerk off thinkin' about it."

Mickey and I said nothing.

"Don't come skulkin' around no more when I'm shacked up," Biff warned us. "Now get your asses *outta* here! Turn around and *run*, goddamn you!"

With Biff's coarse laugh braying after us, Mickey and I ran as hard as we could up the steep zigzag path through the woods, past the orchard, and into the alley. Sweat was pouring out of us when we stopped and tried to catch our breaths.

That night, I did toss and turn thinking about that naked girl, Mary Ann, the first naked girl I had ever seen. But I found her repulsive, not pretty, not sensual, not sexy.

CHAPTER 7

Grace Demick pounded on our front door harder and more frantically than she did on the day Hitler died. Crying and shaking, she exclaimed, "Angie! Ronnie didn't come home from school yesterday! I don't know where he is!"

It was Friday afternoon, Good Friday, my first day of the Easter break from school, and my mom and I had been watching cartoons on our black-and-white TV. We both got to our feet in a hurry. Grace couldn't stand still, and her voice was shaking. She said, "I worked at the concession stand last night and got home late after the movies. Tillman worked a four-to-twelve shift. We thought Ronnie was in bed, and neither checked on him. But this morning, he didn't come down to breakfast."

Tillman Demick opened our front door right then and came in, as upset as Grace was. She wore a faded house dress, and her hair was up in curlers. Tilly was in rumpled brown slacks and a limp, wrinkled T-shirt. My mom and I were just as shaken as they were. Tillman, bigger and more rotund than my father, always had a kindly way about him, and he came over to me as I got up from the couch. I was still in my flannel pajamas, as I often was from breakfast till noon on a Saturday morning. Tilly put his hand on my shoulder and asked in a soft, unthreatening way, "David, if you know where Ronnie went yesterday and who he was with, you can tell me, and you won't be punished even if he was doing something he shouldn't have been doing. I know you boys keep certain secrets from us moms and dads."

"I only know he was supposed to go to Mickey Jenkins's house. In Colonial Village." The "Village" was a collection of homes that cheaply approximated "colonial." They cost a little more than our house and were single-unit, and I thought at the time because I didn't know any better, that they were upscale compared to the duplexes on Farnsworth Avenue.

Tilly asked me, "Do you have Mickey's phone number?" I rattled it off by heart, and he went to use our house phone without asking. It was in the hallway to the upstairs, and my dad had yet to rip it out of the wall lately.

Meantime, my dad came up from the cellar. "What the hell's goin' on?" he barked. "All this goddamn commotion."

When he passed me, I smelled whisky. He was often down in the cellar because that's where he hid his bottle.

"Ronnie's missing, Johnny," Grace told him. "He wasn't in his bed this morning. He's been gone all night long." She once again burst into a flood of tears.

"Holy shit!" was my dad's response.

Tillman got through to Mickey's mother and asked her many questions while the rest of us listened. When he hung up the phone, he shook his head in dismay and said, "Her son Mickey didn't come home either. She says Mickey and Ron were supposed to come over there yesterday after school. Ron was going to help him build a model airplane, but they never showed up. I asked her if Mickey had ever run away from home before, and she said he'd have no reason to do that. She has no idea where he might be."

"My God! Maybe someone kidnapped them!" my mom moaned, and tears were running down her face.

"Jesus Christ! Don't start bawling!" my dad barked. "You want a drink, Tilly?"

My dad's first resort in any crisis, or even a non-crisis, was a slug of whisky. And if Tilly took one, it would give him an excuse to take one too.

But Tilly said, "No, thanks, John. I've got to keep my head straight until I find out where my son is."

Even though they were both alcoholics, Tillman was usually more reasonable than my dad was and far easier to get along with.

"You sure?" my dad persisted.

Tilly again said no.

"Let's go back to our house," he said to Grace. We have to think of some more people who might know something. And we should probably call the police right away."

"Let's wait until we make a couple more phone calls first," Grace said, " before we get the whole town up in arms."

"I'm up in arms right now!" my dad shouted. Any time anything went wrong, he wanted to rip the whole world apart. Tillman and Grace went out the door, and my dad started cursing and pacing around the living room. "I'll betcha any goddamn money that bastard Biff Conley did something to Ronnie and that other boy, what's- his name?"

"Mickey Jenkins," I reminded.

"Ronnie and Mickey! If Biff hurt them in any way, I'll *kill* him! He and his screwed-up buddies! I'll bash their *heads* with the *pipe* I keep in my car! They bunch of goddamn *thugs and bullies!* They should have been *locked away* a long time ago! They got no *respect* for nothin'! Look how they tore all the *brass from* the ground up on Memorial Hill!"

I didn't care to hear anymore, so I quietly eased myself into the hall and up to my room because I knew I was going to cry, and if I did it in front of my dad saw, he'd call me a sissy. I tried to tell myself it was too soon to cry because we didn't yet know that we had any reason to be so stricken. But in my gut, I somehow knew. The circumstances were too strange. I was so sick I could have thrown up. I had never felt such dread.

Four days later, Ron Demick and Mickey Jenkins still had not been found. What was scarier was that a third boy was also missing, and most people were assuming that his disappearance was connected to the other two, but this was not known for sure. I didn't know him as well as I knew Ron and Mickey. His name was Joey Angelo, and he was in seventh grade, a year behind me. At this point, most of my classmates started to say out loud that the three boys must be dead. Almost nobody believed that they had run away. We all realized that they couldn't have had enough money to get far even if they were runaways.

My mother had speculated that they might have been kidnapped because that carried some hope that they might still be alive. But so far as I knew, there was no ransom note. If some pervert had grabbed them, his motive seemed to be something else besides money.

It was all I could do to get through my first day back at school on Monday. I couldn't pay attention in class. I couldn't act average around my friends. At night, I fiddled with my homework without completing it and turning it in. Mostly, I stayed in my room. When I thought I might be able to stop bawling, I forced myself to go to the playground, but it was full of memories of Ron and Mickey, and I choked up and dropped my carom stick and ran. I went into the woods and down to the shack and stayed there by myself for two hours, even though my parents had told me not to go anywhere alone, especially into the woods, while some maniac might be on the loose.

Biff Conley and his gang were still out on bail from their theft of the brass plaques, and gossip around town labeled them suspects in whatever had happened to Ron, Mickey, and Joey. There was a flurry of hopeful excitement when the cops hauled them in for an interrogation, but they were not detained. As soon as they were released, they beat up Herbie Green, a sad, homely, forty-year-old "known queer" who was spotted ogling little kids on the monkey bars. Biff and his buddies bragged that they had made Herbie blow them, apparently believing it did not make *them* queer because they were the blowees. Herbie got a black eye, split lip, broken teeth, and cracked ribs, but he was too scared to press charges.

The school was out from Good Friday through Easter Sunday, which came on April 13th that year. On Saturday, I dragged myself to Confession and told all my sins without fudging so I'd be in what the Church deemed "the perfect State of Grace" while I prayed to Jesus and Mary to let Ron and Mickey come home safe and unharmed. Kneeling in a pew alone and saying my penance, I felt futile, pathetic, and tired. What did God or the universe care about me or my troubles? The evil in the world seemed to be immune to prayers. At age thirteen, I still believed in the tenets of the Catholic religion, but I had a lot of doubt about the integrity of miracles. If the ones described in the Bible had happened, why didn't things like this happen nowadays?

Any shred of hope for a miracle was dashed completely two days after Easter. Ron,

Mickey and Joey were found. But they were dead. That was all my parents told me on that terrible Tuesday when I was thirteen years old. They protected me from the horrific details, but in school, I heard strange, awful rumors that later turned out to be true. The three boys were found stripped naked and submerged in a pond just off a trail about fifty yards from our shack. Their wrists and ankles were bound with their shoelaces. They had cuts and bruises on their arms, legs, and chests. Supposedly, their genitals were missing, which made me shudder and gave me the creeps. I had recurrent nightmares, not only right then but even later in my life.

I could barely believe that Ron and Mickey were gone from my life and always would be, and I felt a tight pain in my heart every time I thought of them. When I knew I was going to break down, I ran upstairs to my room before my dad saw me cry and told me not to be a big sissy. My mother sometimes came in softly and tried to comfort me, but I didn't want her comfort; I just wanted to be left alone.

Somehow, the parents of the murdered boys agreed with each other to hold all three funerals on the same day and in the same Roman Catholic church that my parents and I went to, even though some of them weren't Catholic. I don't know how I got through the whole thing. The liturgy enveloped me, swirling through my mind and body like an inbred nightmare. The church was so packed that the crowd swelled through the doors and into the street. The trip to the cemetery, behind three hearses, was total torture, as was the graveside ceremony with its ending of "Ashes to ashes, dust to dust." Then came the wake in the back room of our American Legion, and for me, it was all a blur.

Two days after the bodies were buried, a homicide detective came to our house. When my mom called me into the living room, I had force-fed myself a peanut butter sandwich and was getting a glass of water to wash it down. "This is Detective Martinelli," she said. "He wants to talk to you." She retreated into the kitchen, and I stood there feeling nervous and awkward. I was glad my father was at work so he couldn't embarrass me by angrily butting into whatever would take place.

The detective had brown wavy hair and a neatly trimmed mustache, and he wore a dark pinstripe suit with a white shirt and a red-and-black striped tie. I realized suddenly that he must be *Vito* Martinelli, one of Clairton High School's legendary athletes. He was in the photo of our 1942 State Champion Football Team in a showcase across from the administration office, along with the trophy they had won. He must be about 28 years old. I knew he had gone to Penn State on a football scholarship, where he had been a starting fullback. I didn't know whether he had been drafted into

40

World War Two. But I was recollecting that I had heard he was now a police officer.

He said, "Let's sit down, David," and we both sat on our small couch. He peered at me so closely that I tried not to squirm.

"I was told you were friends with Ron Demick and Mickey Jenkins," he said. I nodded while I fought back tears.

"What about Joey Angelo?" he asked. "Did you know him?"

"I knew who he was," I managed to say after clearing my throat.

"But you weren't as close to him as you were to the other two boys?"

"He lived down on Reed Street and wasn't in my classes or study periods."

"Did you think maybe he was gay?"

"Some of the guys did."

"Can you think of anybody who might've wanted to hurt him?"

"I don't know," I said hesitantly, remembering what had been done to Herbie Green.

But Detective Martinelli continued as if he had read my thoughts. "Do you know Spencer Conley?"

"You mean Biff?"

"Yeah, Biff Conley."

"He picked on Ron and me, especially Ron. He would punch him and slap him around every time he saw him. I don't know if he ever did that to Joey Angelo."

"We have a witness who says he did," Detective Martinelli revealed. "Do you think I ought to believe her?"

"Who is she?"

"I'm not at liberty to say right now."

I said, "Biff Conley picked on everybody he could. He and the rest of his gang. So, it's not hard to believe they probably picked on Joey, too."

"You younger boys built a log shack in the woods, and I've been told that Biff and his gang of bullies took it over sometimes. The three victims were found close by, as you probably know, because we were unable to keep them from getting out. Do you think they went down there alone, or could they have been lured there?"

I said, "It could have happened either way. I'm not sure that Biff Conley planned any of his bullying. He just took advantage of every opportunity."

"What about their theft of the brass plaques on Memorial Hill?"

"It could have been a spur-of-the-moment thing. Everybody knew the plaques were worth a lot of money at the junkyard. Unlike a bank robbery, going after them could have been on pure impulse. It was a stupid thing to do because any junk dealer would immediately know where the brass markers came from and call the police. Unless they planned to melt them down and fence them."

Martinelli shot me a sharp look. "You're a smart kid. You ever think of becoming a detective?"

"I've thought of trying to write a crime novel," I admitted shyly.

"I hope you do that someday," he said as he got to his feet and buttoned his suit jacket.

"If you think of anything, you should tell me- anything that I haven't thought to ask- and get in touch, day or night." He took a card from his shirt pocket and handed it to me. "Here's my contact information. Don't hesitate to use it."

"I don't want Biff Conley to come after me. Does he have to know you talked to me?"

"No. No. It's not like you were an eyewitness to anything, so there would be no reason for you to testify against him in court."

"I'd help put him away if I could," I said.

"I don't doubt it," Martinelli said. "He hates queers. But if we put him in prison, he's gonna find out he's not the tough guy he thinks he is. He's gonna be down on his knees in front of some big mean dude with his pants down."

"You don't think I'm queer, do you?" I managed to ask as my face reddened. In those days and at that time and place, all of us dreaded any accusation of homosexuality.

Martinelli chuckled and said, "No, don't worry, kid. It never crossed my mind. You don't come across that way."

I was greatly relieved. I didn't know it, but this wouldn't be my last involvement with Detective Martinelli. Years later, when I made my first horror film, *Intensive Scare*, I shot it in Clairton and used Vito as a technical consultant. And on the sequels, which had bigger budgets, I hired him as my chief of security and a technical consultant, and we became close friends. As the years rolled by, and as we trusted each other more and more, he began to share my doubts about whether the murderers of my boyhood friends were the ones who were put in prison or if the guilty ones had gone free.

CHAPTER 8

My grandmother lived by herself in a house that was too big for her in a tiny little borough ironically named Large, PA. It was only a few miles from Clairton, but my mother called it "out in the sticks." In those days, when not so many families had cars, it seemed that way because Grandma Cristi didn't have "city water" or indoor plumbing. She had a cistern and an outhouse. Her husband, Grandpa Felix, who used to beat my dad with a belt buckle, had died of cancer before I was born. When I was thirteen, my grandmother was sixty-three. Her hundred-year-old house had rain-streaked asbestos siding and a concrete porch with six brick pillars. It stood on a half-acre lot with a sprawling lawn, a large garden that she planted and tended all by herself, a sagging garage with a tarpaper roof, and a chicken coop with a wire fence that imprisoned a dozen or so hens and a mean rooster who would give you a severe bite if you stuck your hand through the wall. Grandma Cristi, who wasn't afraid of anything, didn't get too close to that rooster when she entered the coop to grab a hen to kill and pluck. She still drove to Clairton in her 1934 Ford when she needed to buy something, which was rare because she lived off her chickens and eggs, fruit from her peach and apple trees, and vegetables from her garden.

What little I knew about my family history came from her, in broken English. Grandpa Felix came here from Italy at age twenty-five, in 1898, when the Spanish-American War broke out. She arrived in 1901 at age twelve. They met and married in Pittsburgh when he was thirty, and she was fourteen. It was his second marriage. It was rumored that he had killed his first wife when she was pregnant by punching her in her belly. Maybe that's why he fled to Large, PA, which was far removed from big-city civilization in those days. That's where my dad was born, delivered at home by an Italian-speaking midwife.

Grandma Cristi, whose first name was Maria, was not formally educated, but she had "folk wisdom." Around the house, she usually wore an apron over her well-rounded belly, and her long gray hair was bunny. I liked her uninhibited laughter, her no-nonsense investment in a life of hard work, and her excellent peasant-style cooking. Everything was homemade, even the noodles. She would pull and roll the dough into long strands and hang them on clean tea towels over the backs of chairs in her kitchen in the basement. Her tomato sauce was one of the wonders of this world.

I used to bicycle to her place to cut her lawn with a push-mower at least once a week in the summertime. It was hard work and helped me build my muscles before lifting weights. After Ron Demick, Mickey Jenkins, and Joey Angelo were killed, I started bicycling to Grandma's house more often, not just to get farther away from where the murders had happened but also to get away from my parents.

One day in early May of 1952, while the murderers had still not been caught, I rode my bicycle to her house, put my bike on its kickstand to one side of the brick walkway, went onto the porch, and knocked on the screen door. Grandma opened it and gave me a big hug. I could smell her delicious beef and endive soup wafting from the kitchen.

She asked me the same question she usually requested. How's-a da Katzenjammer Kids? They kill each other yet?"

The Katzenjammer Kids was a comic strip in the *Pittsburgh Press* about a German American family with two bratty, mischievous boys who were always fighting, bickering, and playing dastardly tricks on each other and their parents. But their antics were comical, and my parents weren't.

"Still the same," I said to Grandma.

"Notting gonna change," she said solemnly. Then she smiled warmly. "You come in; you eat some good soup. Then you cutta da grass. But you already cutta last-a week."

I said, "Maybe I won't do it again just yet. We'll eat and talk."

"Thatta be nice," she agreed.

We ate and talked, and when we were just about done eating, she said, "You come uppa stairs, I gonna show you somet'ing."

We went up to her bedroom, which had old-fashioned push-button light switches and the same big brass bed that had always been there. She turned on the overhead light and opened a cedar chest under one of the large windows with filmy blue curtains. She took out a tri-folded United States flag, showed it to me, and returned it. Then she took out a little jewelry box, opened it, and handed it to me. It held a Marine Corps ring with the globe and anchor emblem I recognized from the movies.

She said, "I give this to you. It belongs to my brudder. He gotta killed inna Chicago."

"Killed?" I asked. "Do you mean murdered, Grandma?"

"Inna hotel inna Chicago. On three-day pass. Smoddered inna his bed, da legs an' arms tied to bed rungs. Dey caught the man, an' dey let him go free."

She said all this with great bitterness, and I was speechless. I had never heard that we had someone in our family who was murdered.

My grandmother handed me a tiny clipping from a Chicago newspaper, only about an inch and a half long and just a column wide. I read it but didn't see a date on it. It said that Marine Corporal August Cristi was smothered to death in his

46

hotel room, and the prime suspect was a sailor named Michael Stout, who was arrested but freed for lack of evidence.

"What year did this happen?" I asked Grandma.

She said, "He was my younger brudder, twenty-four years old in 1915. Dey letta da bastard go!"

"I'm sorry, Grandma."

Tears rolled down her cheeks, and she bit her lip, drawing blood. I watched her pull a hanky from her apron and dab at the trickle, and I tried not to shed tears but failed, which embarrassed me. She told me not to be ashamed to cry. She said that men and women both had plenty to cry about in this world. "Your poor Uncle August, he fights inna the war 'cause he wanna be 'American. But when he come back 'merica donna care."

What my grandmother told me that day probably had something to do with my burning desire, years later, to get justice for Ron Demick and the other two boys.

CHAPTER 9

Three weeks after the victims' bodies were found, Biff Conley and two members of his gang of five were arrested, and three months after that, in July 1953, they went on trial for kidnapping and murder. The two others pled guilty to the thefts on Memorial Hill but had alibis that pardoned them from the murders. I read in the *Pittsburgh Press* that the coroner had placed the three boys' deaths roughly within the twenty-four hours from the afternoon of the Thursday before Easter to the afternoon of the following day, Good Friday. But since the boys had gone missing on Thursday after school, that left late Thursday afternoon as the likeliest time for the murders, and that was precisely when one of Biff's pals had been seen working in his father's body shop. Another one had been seen running errands for his mother at a grocery store, a drug store, and a dry cleaner. Therefore, all five were held in the Clairton jail until three of them went on trial for the murders, while the other two, who had alibis for the murders, began serving two years in the county prison in Pittsburgh for the thefts.

My father bitched constantly, drunk or sober, about the two who had not been charged with the murders because of what he called "trumped-up alibis." Sometimes, his anger escalated, and he took it out on my mother as if he was punishing the two young thugs who, in his estimation, had gotten away with a triple murder.

Tillman Demick started coming over to our half of the duplex more often to drink on the back porch with my father. One day, after Tilly had staggered home, my father called me down to the basement and told me repeatedly how much I was going to miss him when he died. He hugged me so tightly I couldn't get away from him, making his death sound so sad and imminent that when he finally let me go, I went to my mother with tears on my face.

She said, "Don't worry about him, honey, it's just a crying jag. He won't even remember it when he sobers up."

I had never heard the term "crying jag" and was still severely shaken by seeing my father broken down into one.

"He kept talking about dying," I told my mother. "I'm afraid he has cancer or something and doesn't want us to know."

She chuckled amusedly at that. "He might kill himself with the booze. That's the only kind of sickness *he* has. His crocodile tears are mostly for himself. Alcoholics are full of self-pity, but they rarely change their ways; they keep making their lives miserable and taking it out on the people who love them."

Grace Demick knocked softly on our front door, then let herself in. Like Tillman, she had been coming over more often since Ron's death, in need of my mother's company. They'd have coffee and cookies or cake in the kitchen. They both cried a lot, too. And they shared whatever they had found out about the arrests and the upcoming trial. Grace knew more than my mother did because Vito Martinelli kept in touch with her somewhat. I hung around and listened when they talked. I tried to piece together scraps of information I got from them, comingled with gossip and rumors at school and around town, plus newspaper reports.

Before the murders, I had known little about Biff Conley or his accomplices. I had feared them in the abstract, but I hadn't understood them to any greater extent than the victim of a predatory animal understands its stalker. Now, I was becoming aware of details that were new to me.

At the time of their arrests, Spencer "Biff" Conley was eighteen, Howard "Drummer" Drummond was seventeen, and Maurice "Mo" Brubaker was nineteen. In addition to being charged for the thefts on Memorial Hill, Conley, and Drummond had previous arrests for vandalism and shoplifting, and Brubaker had been expelled from school for assaulting a gym teacher.

Although the oldest of the three, Brubaker was the most childlike. His IQ was in the low eighties. He only passed eighth and ninth grades once he repeated them in summer school. He would have failed tenth and eleventh grades if tutors did not aid him and students that he bullied into helping him cheat. Two of his teachers anonymously admitted that they had turned a blind eye so he could be moved on and they wouldn't have to deal with him anymore. They said he was failing twelfth grade and would not have graduated even if he had not been expelled.

To my surprise, I found out that Howard Drummond had made good grades in high school, had shown art talent, and had been encouraged to try to go to college and study interior design. His teachers believed he could have become a productive citizen had he not fallen in with Spencer Conley. They found it hard to believe that he had succumbed to such a bad influence, and they were at a loss to explain it.

Biff had been raised by a brutally strict father and an alcoholic mother. Social workers repeatedly came into his home to observe the situation and report on it, but for some reason, they refrained from placing him into Child Protective Services. In his early teens, he frequently ran away, and as an adolescent, he had spent brief periods in a psychiatric ward in Pittsburgh. He dropped out of school when he was sixteen and worked off and on as a burger flipper. He told the police that his mother and father took most of the money he earned, and his father often hit him with his fists, whether he had done anything to deserve it.

Up until the time of the murders, I could have empathized with the three of them if I hadn't been so afraid of them. But now I hated them. I wanted them to get the death penalty, which at that time in Pennsylvania meant the electric chair. And I wanted them to be executed swiftly, not after years and years on Death Row. I did not doubt that it was what they deserved for killing my friends.

CHAPTER 10

The trial became a national sensation when the prosecutors declared in their opening argument that the three defendants were Satanists and that the jury would be hearing the hard evidence to prove it. Clairton wasn't in the Bible Belt and wasn't a hotbed of fanatical religion and superstition. Still, when it hit the news that a belief in Satanism was a possible motive for the murders, my little hometown was swarmed by all the news outlets, from the *Pittsburgh Press* and the *McKeesport Daily News* to media giants like *Time* and *Newsweek*, plus the local radio and TV stations and the major networks. It became common for us to spot talking heads who were great celebrities to us in the streets or bars and restaurants.

A spokesperson from NBC wanted to interview me as a friend of two of the murder victims, and my mother would have given her consent, but my dad wouldn't allow it. I didn't know if I was relieved or disappointed.

I read in the *Daily News* an opinion piece surmising that the prosecution had wanted to

hit the jury with the Satanism angle to put that strange and shocking motive in the minds of the jury right at the outset. They bolstered it by calling a psychiatrist as one of their first witnesses.

Dr. Gabriel Horner had treated Spencer "Biff" Conley in the psychiatric ward at McKeesport Hospital. He testified that Biff suffered from "a serious mental illness characterized by grandiose persecutory delusions, auditory and visual

52

hallucinations, disordered thought processes, substantial lack of insight, and chronic incapacitating mood swings." His most recent interaction with the patient had been only three months ago, and during one of the sessions, Biff claimed that he obtained special powers by drinking human blood. Still, when the doctor asked him if he had ever done so, he rambled inconclusively.

When Detective Vito Martinelli took the stand, he said that the condition of the three victims had caused him to think that the crime seemed to have "cult overtones." This line of thinking was enhanced when he learned that Spencer Conley, the pack's leader, was a self-proclaimed witch or devil worshiper who might easily have influenced his pals in that direction.

The most startling revelation from Detective Martinelli was that during one of his interrogations, Conley had mumbled that the murdered boys had wounds to their genitals. But Biff had clammed up, going wary suddenly and babbling incoherently when asked to describe the lacerations. Nothing of the genital mutilations had ever been publicly released, and even though it had been verified by observation and by autopsy, Conley should not have known about it unless he had been there and seen it when it had happened.

Because of these salient points and much more evidence and testimony during the trial, the jury had ample reason to believe that the three defendants were guilty. And so did I. At that time and for long afterward, I took grim satisfaction in the fact that they were speedily convicted and that Biff was condemned to death and the other two got sentences of forty years in prison. As the years rolled by, I kept up as best I could with the many appeals and requests for new trials, and for a long time, no new evidence came forward, and they stayed in prison. Each decision that went against them made me want to cheer. I was dismayed when I read a short column in the

Pittsburgh Press claiming that Mary Ann Sumpter, the girl everyone knew that Biff was having sex with down at our shack, had recanted the testimony she had given at trial, which had placed Biff near where the murders had taken place, and within the exact time frame to help prove his guilt. But now, according to Biff's attorney, Mary Ann would change her story. I kept watching for an update on that disturbing development, but nothing ever materialized, so far as I could discover, and the possibility faded away. Little did I know that it would resurface years later and change everything, including my own certainty about the convictions.

CHAPTER 11

After the emotional anguish of the trial, I tried to push the murders out of my mind.

There was a side of me that didn't want close friends anymore for fear of losing them the way I had lost Ron and Mickey. I became reclusive compared to how gregarious I used to be.

I saved up some money from getting five bucks from my parents for getting good grades on my report cards, and I used it to buy a set of barbells and dumbbells that I kept in the basement. I wanted to get bigger and stronger, so I'd be less likely to be picked on by bullies like Biff Conley. I used the weights a lot, or else I stayed in my room studying and reading or trying to, but repeatedly, I was tormented by unbidden thoughts of drowned and mutilated bodies.

One day, I tried to escape the torment by leaving the house and riding my bike up a steep hill, hoping to tire myself out so much that I might be able to fall asleep that night. The hill leveled out and became Malmedy Village, a street of low-cost homes converted from World War Two army barracks and named for a town in France where the Nazis massacred eighty-four American prisoners of war. The houses had no basements because the barracks had been built on concrete slabs, and my dad had said they were cheaper to buy than the duplexes on Farnsworth Avenue and mainly were for returning veterans.

I had stopped pumping my bike and was sweating and breathing hard when a boy came onto his front porch and yelled, "You're David Cristi!"

I recognized him and yelled back, "You're Jimmy Costello!" I knew his name because he and Ron Demick had been in the same homeroom, and Ron had pointed him out one day at the playground, saying, "He's pretty bright and a really good artist."

"Wanna play football?" Jimmy called out. "Me and a bunch of kids are gonna play after school on Monday!"

I said sure, I wanted to play, and I showed up on the day of the pickup game, not knowing any of the kids on either team. I wanted badly to impress this gang of strangers and not come off like a wimp. Luckily, Jimmy picked me on his team, with him as quarterback. He was a big, strong, good-looking kid who loved being the leader and showing off his great athletic ability. In the first play, he tossed a long bomb, and I raced for it, even though it was way over my head and everybody else's. To my great surprise -- and theirs -- I must've gotten a burst of adrenaline because the tips of my fingers snagged the ball, and I went for a touchdown! All the kids on my team cheered and pounded me on the back for making what they all thought was an impossible catch. I remember that moment with pride and disbelief to this day.

Jimmy Costello became one of my most admired and treasured friends, and it turned out that by the time we were ready to graduate from high school, we had shyly discovered that we both wanted to become writers. This was a rare aspiration in Clairton, where most guys our age were happy to get a job in the steel mills. My parents were pressuring me to go to college and not end up in the kind of job my father had wound up in and hated so much. At the same time, they were desperate for me to land a scholarship because they couldn't afford the costs. In succeeding summers, I had worked as a janitor's helper and a basket-checker at the swimming pool, but I only made ninety cents an hour, which didn't amount to a hill of beans when it came to saving money.

I worked my butt off making the Honor Roll during my senior year, and my parents bragged about me no end when I actually did land a scholarship provided by a local chemical corporation that annually donated ten two-thousand-dollar scholarships to graduating seniors based on academic status and financial need. I was helped by the fact that my dad only made about $6,000 per year as a top-rated millwright. That wasn't great money even in those days when a new car only cost about $3,000, and a middle-class home could be bought for $10,000.

To claim the scholarship, I had to prove that a university had accepted me, so I enrolled at West Virginia University. The year before the murders, Ron Demick and his parents had invited me on a trip to WVU to visit his cousin at the agricultural school, and I fell in love with the beautiful campus. I didn't want to commute to Pitt because that would have meant long, smelly bus rides back and forth every day, and my parents would have been constantly looking over my shoulder to ensure I was studying. I didn't want to give up a chance to escape their fights and arguments. Because my favorite high school teachers inspired me, I majored in English education even though teachers were ridiculously underpaid. I had a powerful urge to become a published novelist someday and hoped that courses in literature and creative writing would help me toward that goal. Jimmy Costello had enrolled at Carnegie Institute of Technology as a fine arts major. Still, he wasn't there on scholarship because his high-school grades were too low, not from a low IQ but from a lack of willingness to study or do homework. I was near the end of my first semester at WVU when he phoned with the shocking news that he had dropped out of college. "I was flunking anyway," he said. "I didn't want to draw things they told me to draw instead of doing my own thing. I got an F for drawing a scene from *Viva Zapata* when I was supposed to draw a skinny young girl posing nude in front of the room. My dad is all bent out of shape. He threatened to take my car keys and kick me out of the house. I told him I wanted to enroll at the Pittsburgh Playhouse and take courses on the side from the Pittsburgh Filmmakers Association. He said that if I don't knuckle down and get a degree that'll land me a job, I won't be worth the powder to blow me up. But he didn't kick me out, and two days later, he gave me back my car keys. He said he'd pay for one year of me acting like a beatnik, and I damn well better get it out of my system because after that, he'll cut me loose, and I'll have to make it on my own."

"What did your mom say about it?" I asked.

"Nothing. She stood slightly behind my father, nodding to show me she agreed with everything he said."

Jimmy's parents had the money to rightly or wrongly indulge Jimmy's little flings with "irresponsibility." Still, my parents didn't have much money or patience with that kind of what they would've called "monkey business." I had to "keep my nose to the grind" whether I wanted to or not. I envied my friend's burst of what seemed like a carefree kind of freedom. He'd be acting, writing scenes for plays or movies, and learning filmmaking while I was stuck doing nothing, especially adventurous or unique. But during semester breaks or summer breaks from WVU, I hung out with Jimmy and his new friends at every chance. I tagged along when they were rehearsing for plays they were in, attending plays that their friends were in, or going to art houses to watch foreign films that we thought were vastly superior to the Doris Day and Rock Hudson fluff Hollywood was cranking out. We loved the British *Carry on* comedies, the Ingmar Bergman ensemble films like *The Virgin Spring*, the serious Italian movies like *La Dolce Vita* and *La Strada* and laughed our butts off at *Big Deal on Madonna Street*.

58

Jimmy had made a special friend named Brent Julian, who was already landing speaking parts in some of the plays at the Playhouse. When he was learning his lines, he spotted them with great enthusiasm -- and quite loudly -- anywhere and everywhere that we happened to be, even in crowded upscale restaurants. He did an excellent job with Hamlet's soliloquy.

But it almost got us kicked out of a theater where a Road Runner cartoon was showing. Jimmy and I talked energetically and enthusiastically about artistic and creative things and social, political, and cultural issues. Still, there also was very little about our personal lives that we didn't share. That included the murders of the three boys in Clairton. I confessed that I still had horrible nightmares. I could open up to Jimmy Costello and Brent Julian without fear that they wouldn't understand or make fun of me. We felt that our friendship was special and holy, and this was powerfully liberating for three callow but innately talented adolescents still trying to find themselves. There was great joy in seeing that we were on the same wavelength about many things that others would undervalue, mock, or have no interest in.

In the summer heading into my junior year at WVU, I started writing a series of sketches about the nutty and dangerous escapades that we Farnsworth kids had indulged in, such as us fooling around with gunpowder and blasting caps, our shack building, our fist fighting, and our battles with rocks, spears, and clubs like Knights of the Sandlot. Brent and Jimmy read my first ten or fifteen sketches, and Jimmy thought they were too disconnected and needed a unifying theme with fewer characters, just two or three in a suspenseful conflict. But Brent said he had gotten a kick out of each story, and I could make them hang together like the tapestry of vignettes in John Steinbeck's *Cannery Row*. I was flattered and encouraged by that comment because *Cannery Row* and *Tortilla Flat* were the works I had been inspired by and hoped to emulate.

Jimmy said I should write about the murders because they were the most riveting, unique events of my life, but I said I wasn't ready to do that yet.

He said, "It might be therapeutic, you know?"

But even thinking about putting my scary thoughts down on paper scared *me*, so I said, "Maybe I'll do it someday, but not now."

I didn't know that "someday" would be decades. I think I was suffering from post-traumatic stress syndrome without having a label for it. Back then, we called it "shell shock," but we didn't think it applied to civilians, just soldiers. Our high school guidance counselor, Peter Houlihan, was said to be shell-shocked because he had suffered through massive bombing attacks in the Battle of the Bulge. Some of the crueler students called him "Shaky Pete." They would drop books on the classroom floor with a loud crash, making him jump and shake and stifle their giggles with their hands over their mouths. Biff Conley used to get his rocks off doing that, and he'd laugh uproariously, boasting about it to us younger kids.

Back then, I tried hard to wipe Biff's memory out of my life, but it kept coming back and haunting me at almost every turn. The three convicted killers were currently waiting for a decision on one of their appeals, and I was dreading it. I did not doubt that they were guilty. If they weren't, why hadn't there been more of the same kind of murders?

When I had enough sketches to make a book of about 50,000 words, I submitted it to a string of publishers under a rather silly-sounding title: Duckworth Avenue instead of Farnsworth Avenue because I didn't know if using the name of an actual place was legal. Well, it didn't matter anyway because the manuscript just kept piling up rejection slips and coming back to me in the mail, each time getting my hopes up until I opened the package.

I was back at WVU that autumn when Jimmy Costello phoned me with the astounding news that he and Brent Julian had gotten a loan from his uncle in the fantastic amount of $2,000 to make a sixteen-millimeter movie. Oh, boy, was I jealous! I was seventy-five miles from Pittsburgh, where all the action took place! I felt like I was missing out on *everything!*

The movie was to be called *The Mill Town Boys*. It was to be a series of vignettes, some humorous and some deadly serious, and they had been inspired to use that format after reading Duckworth Avenue and hating that title. They figured that for people as inexperienced as we were, creating short pieces would be easier than creating a ninety-minute feature film with a hard-hitting plot and intriguing characters that had to make an audience hang in for the long haul. They wanted me to help convert some of my stories into short screenplays, and they said they'd give me screen credit. I was so flattered and excited I couldn't sleep. I stayed up writing night after night.

At the same time, there was no way I could afford to drop out of WVU, so I hung in there, wishing at every moment, no matter what I was doing on campus or in class, that I could have been with Brent and Jimmy while they were shooting. I took advantage of every moment I could during semester breaks or summer vacations. I helped as much as possible and tried to learn as much as possible about filmmaking. I appeared in one of the sketches as an extra and worked with the crew on several others. The movie bug badly bit me. Now, I not only wanted to become a published author, but I also wanted to become a filmmaker.

One night after we were done shooting, a joint was passed around at a wine-and-pizza bull session, and I found out later that the marijuana was laced with PCP, a chemical known on the street as Angel Dust. I went on a bad trip that almost landed me in an emergency room. I was completely freaking out, feeling myself being sliced, stabbed, and castrated -- and it all felt *real!* Brent, Jimmy, and two other guys had to hold me down, and in my fitful delusions, I was imbued with such strength that I kept bucking and heaving, super strong enough to almost throw them off me.

I finally came out of it and calmed down. But I swore off from marijuana and hash and didn't smoke any for over a year. But eventually, I came back to it and smoked it every day for about a decade without having another lousy trip. Even now, as old as I am, I'll take a toke if it's around, at a party or something, but I don't keep it in my house all the time like I used to when I was young.

Back in the 1960s, there was a pop icon named Timothy Leary who convinced a lot of people that peyote, hash, LSD, and other psychedelics were a means to enhance ESP and other esoteric comprehensions. But when I was deep into that bad trip, I wasn't visited by profound trance-like revelations about the murders. All I got was a deep, ugly sense of what it might have been like to be a victim of such horror.

I reflected on the brutal aspects of growing up in a rough, brawling mill town. There were plenty of funny or adventurous things we did when we were kids on Farnsworth Avenue, and there were also quite a few malicious things that we laughed at when we shouldn't have. Often, our fun got too rough, callous, and crude, but that did not deter our belly laughs. As I matured away from my childhood, I wondered if our zany recklessness might have been a fertile breeding ground for darker forces just under the surface that could escalate in sinister ways, as in *The Lord of the Flies*, a movie that Jimmy Costello and I once saw in a downtown Pittsburgh art house, about kids marooned on an island without their parents, and unwittingly descending into depravity and murder.

One of my sketches that I converted into a screenplay for our movie, *Mill Town Boys*, was a rather prescient look at the problem of bullying, which wasn't getting much attention, if any, back in the sixties. The main characters were Biff Conley, Howard Drummond, and Mo Brubaker, plus a timid little boy named Willy Jacobs that they had picked on unmercifully until one day, he was found drowned in the Clairton swimming pool. A lifeguard got to him, pulled him out of the water, and desperately tried to revive him, but it was useless. He vomited up pieces of a hot dog while the lifeguard was doing CPR and crying his eyes out.

His death was ruled an accident and thought to be due to a cramp while swimming.

But I had sat on a bench and watched Biff and his buddies brutally grab Willy Jacobs in a full nelson, ducking him over and over and making him spit and cry and beg them to stop, but they kept forcing him under, scarcely giving him time to catch a breath, while I slinked away from that bench and berated myself for not having the guts to tell on them.

Jimmy and Brent loved that short story and the screenplay I wrote based on it. They laughed with genuine pleasure because they thought it was one of the vignettes that would give the movie real depth. But writing it wasn't cathartic for me in any way; instead, it required me to wallow in my guilt and try once again to push it out of my mind.

Back when Willy Jacobs had been found floating face-down in the Clairton swimming pool, I couldn't help suspecting that his drowning wasn't accidental. I knew I might have witnessed the lead-up without trying to help him. And now, guiltily looking back on it, I couldn't ignore the implications that it was a precursor to what Biff Conley Howie Drummond and Mo Brubaker had done to Ron Demick.

CHAPTER 12

The Mill Town Boys didn't finish because Brent and Jimmy ran out of money. They tried holding presentations where they showed potential investors the edited picture without sound while acting out the scenes by speaking into a microphone. However, they needed to raise more money to add music and effects and create a finished print. Temporarily discouraged, they grumbled that wealthy "Pittsburgh money guys would rather invest in a ball-bearing factory than a movie." Yet, the city was less provincial than it made it out to be. It was the home of the first Nickelodeon, commercial radio station, and public TV station.

But there was a deep recession in the early sixties, and a war in Colombia resulted in teachers getting drafted right off the job. Therefore, when I graduated from college with my degree in English Education, nobody wanted to hire me because I hadn't served my time in the military. My mother and father were both picking on me, making my life miserable because I wasn't earning any money. So, I went to the Draft Board in McKeesport and signed papers to get it over with.

My departure date for Fort Jackson, South Carolina, was May 1, 1962. After the aborted post-production of The Mill Town Boys, Jimmy Costello and Brent Julian formed a fledgling film company and rented a shabby store-front office for fifty bucks a month. Jimmy had graduated from acting school at the Pittsburgh Playhouse, hoping to become a successful stage actor, but just like me, he had been bitten by the movie bug. He and Brent, who had dropped any desire for more formal education, hoped they could make money by making TV spots till they could succeed as feature filmmakers.

Three days before I left for the army, Jimmy Costello drove me to their shabby and dismal business place, which they had grandiosely named New American Films. My draft notice had come, and I wanted to say goodbye to both, but before we climbed into Jimmy's Plymouth convertible, he grabbed a carton of Pepsis from his mother's fridge and popped a big bag of popcorn. He said, "Gotta bring this to Brent. He hasn't had anything to eat for three days."

While Brent ate the popcorn and Jimmy and I drank Pepsis, they promised me that if they did well when I got out of the army, I'd be welcome to come and work with them. I clung to that unlikely, seemingly preposterous promise through the next two years, even during the Cuban Missile Crisis when it seemed inevitable that we were going to war with the Soviet Union and I would be lucky if I didn't get killed in a Cuban jungle.

About three months before my release from the army, I started getting long, rambling letters from Jimmy that pulsed with excitement over how well he and Brent were doing with their little company: "New American Films is thriving like mad. We're making tons of TV spots even though we hate doing them. Brent now fancies himself to be a whiz kid. He's wearing Brooks Brothers suits and talking Madison Avenue ad-babble during the day, brandishing a fat cigar and acting out his evening madness as an escape while we ascend into the tongue-wag-money-world-of-green-smelling-success. We now have a receptionist and two guys working for us on film crews. We even have a Volksbus to carry our equipment. (And we *own* equipment.) The business is flying up as fast as any business could -- it might even be breaking speed records."

These fantastically upbeat letters from Jimmy made me itch and burn even more, and I had a genuine desire to get back home and start working with him and Brent. Even though I was an army "short-timer" down to my last months and weeks, my time in the military seemed like it would never be over. I had a calendar taped inside my locker, and the bright spot of each morning was when I used a black felt marker to cross out one more day that crept by in slow agony.

Three weeks before my time was up, I got a letter from my mom informing me that my grandmother had passed away suddenly from a heart attack in her kitchen. The Jewel Tea man had found her on one of his regular rounds. I think it's defunct now, but back then, a Jewel Tea man went in a brown truck full of company products and special offers once a month from house to house, neighborhood after neighborhood. My grandmother had been collecting dinnerware, one piece a week, plates, cups, saucers, and soup bowls with the Jewel Tea emblem. Nowadays, collectors will pay a lot of money for that stuff.

My mom's letter informed me of Grandma's passing, and she apologized for not letting me know sooner, but she said that she and my dad had decided not to make me fly home for the funeral since I'd be coming home soon anyway. I respected their decision, partly because I no longer believed in prayers and funerals and partly because I didn't think I could have gotten a three-day pass or an emergency leave.

I wrote back to my mom, expressing my sorrow and assuring her that she and my dad had done the right thing. But my cherished memories of Grandma kept me awake in my bunk for quite a few of my final nights at Fort Bragg, tossing and turning and regretting that I wasn't ever going to spend any more time with her.

I narrowly squeaked out of my time in the army before the Vietnam War heated up and became an immense tragedy that put the names of 58,000 Americans on a black granite wall. The war raged on and on with substantial body counts, and there were massive peace demonstrations all over the country. Jimmy, Brent, and I joined in on a peace march in Pittsburgh, and I helped them film it, thinking the footage might be helpful in some future projects.

I was now in the army reserves and was fearful of getting called up again, and so were prospective employers in the education system and elsewhere. To my great dismay, I was again having difficulty landing a job. It was almost as if I hadn't already served in the military.

When I had first gotten back home, I had hoped that there would be a place for me with Jimmy and Brent at New American Films, as they had once promised, but the reality of their situation was a bit different than Jimmy's bombastic ramblings. Like many other businesses, they were still struggling but trying to maintain a good front. They couldn't afford to hire me and train me. And I still needed help getting a teaching job. My mom and dad were hassling me, and their arguments and fights were escalating. My dad called me a flop. My mother, who usually stuck up for me, now taunted me, saying, "Those who can't do, teach."

Finally, Jimmy and Brent came to my rescue in the fall of 1964 by putting in a good word about me with the head of broadcast production at Ketchum McCleod & Grove, a top ad agency for which New American Films was currently making television commercials. I was hired as an apprentice copywriter. This wasn't my heart's desire, but there was an outside hope that it might get me closer to becoming a movie maker.

One day, while I was still trying to fit in at Ketchum, I was surprised by a phone call from

Vito Martinelli. He told me that Biff Conley's death sentence had been commuted to life in prison, and now he had filed a motion for a new trial. The prosecution would argue against it, and they wanted me to testify.

"Testify to what?" I said, thinking that since nobody had wanted me to provide any testimony at the original trial, why would they want me as a witness now?

"They can't come up with all the witnesses they wanted," Vito told me, "So they're hoping you can add something to their arguments."

"They don't want me to make something up, do they?"

Vito chuckled and said, "No, they'd never ask you to do that."

I said, "Seriously. I don't know anything important. Do I?"

"You know Biff's history of constantly picking on Ron Demick, kicking him, hitting him. It goes to motive. It shows he hated Ron for no reason. You witnessed that. It can make the Appeals Board see that he was predisposed to committing murder. He flipped out big time that day. And his fascination with Satanism played into it."

I mulled it over and said, "I suppose I should do it if you think it might help. I'd do just about anything to keep Biff and the other two in jail where they belong."

"Right now, we're only concerned with Biff," Vito told me. "Howard and Maurice are hanging back on advice from their attorneys, waiting to make their follow-up moves if Conley succeeds. Can you meet with me and the prosecutors in Clairton this evening? At the Municipal Building?"

I agreed, and we set a time.

I was still living with my parents because even though my ad agency job paid a hundred bucks more a month than a teaching job would have, it wasn't nearly as much as my father was making in the mill. But the fact that I had a real job and went to work wearing a suit and tie each day made my college education more worthwhile in my parents' eyes. They were prouder of me and had been arguing a little less lately. However, I was under no illusion that their unacknowledged

68

truce would last. Something would set them off again, no doubt.

I seldom caught sight of Tillman or Grace Demick anymore. They seemed to hide in the house these days and rarely ventured out. They had talked about going "back home" to West Virginia, but Tillman was only in his fifties, too young for a pension, so he had to keep his job. Every payday, he would buy six bottles of Four Roses, line them up on the windowsill in the kitchen, and "nurse" from them till the following payday when they would be gone, and he'd be ready for four new bottles.

I always used every opportunity to avoid the duplex's melancholy atmosphere, so I went straight from work to the meeting with Vito and the prosecutors. It had been twelve years since I had seen Vito, and he had aged well; his hair was gray, but he was still trim and athletic looking. He complimented me, saying, "You're not the skinny little kid I remember anymore. The army must've been good for you." He introduced me to the two attorneys who were to argue in front of the Appeals Board the following week, and neither one was in as good shape as he and I were; one was short and fat, and the other was tall and chubby. They questioned me to find out if I could provide any further testimony against Biff Conley besides the times I had seen him and his gang beating up on Ron Demick, and I told them about the time Biff and his gang had given me and Ron Pink bellies.

They didn't laugh; they nodded and said they'd try to allow it in. I considered revealing my suspicion that they had caused Willy Jacobs to drown, but I held back because just thinking about it again made me feel guilty and ashamed.

They prepped me on how the proceedings would unfold and how I should phrase my testimony, especially on cross-examination. When I got out of there, I was in a shaky, depressed mood from having to dredge up ugly memories that I preferred to keep buried, so I stopped for a beer or two at the Village Inn, a neighborhood bar three blocks from our house on Farnsworth Avenue.

Back then, most of the neighborhood saloons in our town sold ten-ounce drafts for ten cents a glass, which was good because I only had about fifteen dollars in my wallet. The drafts were cold and foamy, and I downed three of them quickly and would have started to relax, except a guy I didn't know was giving me the evil eye from the other end of the bar. Most of the patrons were guys young and old from Farnsworth Avenue and other nearby streets, some playing euchre in a booth, some playing shuffleboard, and some just chatting or watching a baseball game between the Pirates and the Cardinals.

After chugging down those three drafts, I had to go to the men's room, so I got up and headed that way. But the guy who had been staring at me got off from his stool and blocked the aisle. He wasn't much bigger than I was, but he was grizzled and had a mean snarl. He was wearing a limp and dirty denim shirt with the sleeves rolled up, and I could see that his forearms were thick, complex, and hairy. He took off his greasy baseball cap and tossed it on the bar, revealing a sunburned bald pate with a scar that ran from the top of his head to his forehead.

He growled, "I know who you *are*, Mister Fancy Pants, and I was told you're gonna *testify* against my *son!"*

A guy dressed pretty much the same way he was, who had been sitting next to him, got off his stool and stood beside him shoulder to shoulder. They glowered at me and menacingly rolled their husky shoulders.

I knew I was probably going to be punched. Or worse. I glanced around quickly. Most of the other patrons stared at us, interrupting their card game. But I didn't see anybody likely to step in to stop an impending fight or take my part. I was in good shape, thanks to just getting out of the army, plus I was still exercising with weights in the cellar at home. But that didn't mean I could take on two stocky guys simultaneously.

"My son didn't kill *nobody!*" the guy barked at me while I was still trying to digest the fact that he was Biff's father.

In a bar fight, whoever strikes first usually wins. Especially if he does it with a cue stick or a beer bottle. There weren't any cue sticks because there wasn't a pool table, and the nearest beer bottle was my own, so I left it on the bar. I thought of grabbing a shuffleboard puck and smashing Conley in the mouth, which would probably knock his front teeth out and split his lips. But if I did that, and the cops came and arrested all three of us, I'd be the one who got fined or jailed.

While this was going through my head, somebody yelled my name, and I glanced away for a second, which was stupid, and Biff's father sucker-punched me hard right in my jaw and knocked me against the shuffleboard. And while I was sprawled there face down, he started punching me in my kidneys. I went down hard onto the dirty, uncarpeted floor, and he kicked me in my ribs.

The bartender, a skinny young guy in his twenties, ran over to us, brandishing a baseball bat. "Hey! *Hey!*" he yelled. "Get yer asses outta here, or I'm gonna *bash* you before I call the cops!"

Two more punches to my kidneys, and then Biff Conley's dad left the bar with his backup guy right behind him.

I got to my feet, groaning.

Through my pain, I was more determined than ever to testify against Biff in his quest for a retrial, and I made up my mind to lay it on thick. The hearing wasn't until the following week, which gave me time for my kidneys to heal. But not my pride. Whether you get beat up by one guy or a dozen, it carries a humiliation not too different from what Ron and I used to feel when Biff and his boys set

71

upon us. It seemed like the ugly aftereffects of the murders weren't ever going to leave me. Whenever I felt like I was moving on, something crept out of the past to disavow me of that wishful notion. This time, Vito Martinelli wanted me to help block Biff Conley's motion for a new trial. Well, if I had harbored any reservations about that, they went away when his father beat the hell out of me.

A week later, I was still moving slowly and painfully when I went to the hearing with Vito.

He asked what my problem was, and I told him I had a run-in at a bar without saying where or with whom. The hearing was at the Court House on Grant Street in Pittsburgh, a massive tower of pale-yellow stone built in the late 1800s and named for General Grant, whose Scottish troops had been defeated by the French and their Iroquois allies when they attacked Fort Duquesne in the French and Indian War. I majored in English education with a minor in American history, so I knew that when the English finally did capture the fort, after the French had abandoned it, they found the heads of one hundred of Grant's Highlanders impaled on wooden stakes, with their kilts dangling underneath. The English renamed the fort after William Pitt, the British prime minister, and that's how Pittsburgh got its name.

I didn't get to see or hear much of what went on at the hearing while the motion for retrial was being argued because I was allowed to be brought in when it was time for me to do my bit. Then I got a pretty good look at Biff, who was now thirty-one years old and had been in prison for twelve years. He had either mellowed out some or was doing a good act, likely the latter. Even under his orange jumpsuit, his jail-yard muscles were apparent, but his face was sallow due to the lack of sunlight. He kept his head bowed, and his shoulders slumped, trying to appear meek and humble.

As it turned out, even though I had revenge as a motive, I was too honest to fudge my testimony. I told the truth all the way, and I don't know if I was effective, but in any case, Biff didn't get his retrial, which suited me fine. It was payback for all those times Ron and I had been bullied. Payback for those Pink Bellies. And, most of all, payback for murder.

CHAPTER 13

By the spring of 1967, I had worked on many scripts for low-budget TV spots and had been on dozens of sets and locations to watch those scripts being filmed, which was an agency policy when they were grooming a lowly copywriter for bigger things. By observing closely and asking pertinent questions whenever I could, I learned a lot about the filmmaking process. I wasn't an expert yet, but I wasn't a total novice.

My boss at Ketchum was Rocco Di Fabio, who had been transferred to Pittsburgh from the agency's New York headquarters. His big claim to fame was that he had come up with what I had to admit was a great slogan for Schaeffer's beer campaign: *The One Beer to Have when You're Having More Than One!* I remember seeing it splashed all over billboards a couple of years ago. But Rocco must've gotten lucky with that one because his transfer to Pittsburgh was an obvious demotion. He was a short, roly-poly guy with a long, sharp nose and a shock of stiff, brittle-looking, dyed-black hair. He seemed tired and worn out by years in the agency game, but he thoroughly knew film production, and I learned a lot from him. He told me, "If you don't know camerawork, lighting, editing, and all the other stuff, you can't write for it. Your concepts won't fly unless the director saves your ass."

In the summer of that year, Pittsburgh independent filmmakers George Romero and Russ Streiner were gearing up to shoot a little horror film on a shoestring budget. Rocco Di Fabio had hired them for some Iron City beer spots shot at the

Seven Springs ski resort the previous winter, so I had met them on location and got along well with them, although I wouldn't say we were bosom buddies. They were competitors for gigs that Jimmy Costello and Brent Julian tried to get but usually didn't because they got trumped by George and Russ's company, The Latent Image. We had heard they had brought their little feature film off the ground on just $6,000, mostly borrowed from friends, families, and finance companies. They didn't even have a title, so they called it a "Monster Flick." Rocco called it "a shitty little horror film," and Jimmy and Brent pooh-poohed it because they were jealous. Who could've known it would be *Night of the Living Dead?*

New American Films was floundering during its short existence, then went out of business in 1970. Brent landed on his feet, so to speak, because he was put into a cushy job in his father's insurance company, and Jimmy's money worries were alleviated when he married Jeannie Loffler, a lovely and utterly sensible woman ten years older than he was, who had a high-paying job as an executive secretary at IBM. She kept him in a lavish apartment just outside the city proper and made no effort to get a job. Instead, he was writing a novel, convinced it would make him rich and famous, leading to a big-time movie deal. I would periodically be invited to dinner by Jimmy and Jeannie, and I would drink wine and read his manuscript as it progressed, then offer suggestions. I thought it was a fabulous piece of writing, and I could see why Jimmy believed it would rescue him from a mundane existence. He said, "Fuck that piece-of-crap monster film George and Russ are making; I want to do serious work, not shit work."

I didn't foresee that this was the beginning of Jimmy pulling away from those of us who had been his allies and friends. He succumbed to living off his wife's income while pipe-dreaming that he was destined to become a big-time author. And she seemed to believe in him as much as he did.

He had a charisma that had snowed her when they first started dating and continued to snow her ever after. All through grade school, high school, and for several years more, I had firmly believed that he and I would be best friends forever, but in just a few short years, the hard knocks, disillusion, and disappointment of what was called "real life" had made his friendship flake away and turn into bitterness. I could see that he still had dreams and ambitions but needed more drive and persistence. His jealousy and anger at the world's refusal to bow to his talent rose to a fever pitch when George Romero's little "monster flick," despite all the odds stacked against it, became a monster hit and a significant groundbreaker.

When *Night of the Living Dead* had its world premiere on October 1, 1968, I had just started dating a charmer named Danielle Stanwix, and she was so scared through the movie that she squeezed my hand till I thought she might break it. I sat there, enduring the pain in more ways than one. I was glad for George Romero, and I had no question about that, but I was regretful that I was a mere observer of his success and not part of it.

Danielle sensed what was troubling me. As I drove her to her apartment across the river from the theater, she said, "You wanted to be involved with that movie."

"I guess so," I admitted. "I maybe could've gotten in on it somehow if I wasn't working at Ketchum."

"You have to do what's in your heart. And your heart isn't in the ad game. If you don't find a way to do what you love doing, you'll never be happy."

We were dating on the sly because her father, Jim Stanwix, was an account manager at Ketchum, and she was in the secretary pool. The agency had a policy against employees getting too cozy with one another; in other words, "Don't put your Peter on the payroll." We laughed and derided the crassness of it, but we could both lose our jobs if we got caught.

I met Danielle when Rocco Di Fabio and I were producing intermission trailers to hawk hotdogs and popcorn at a chain of drive-ins. She was a bright, perky, natural blonde, and I sneakily asked her to go out with me. We kept on furtively dating for about five months, and then we got secretly engaged, still worried about keeping our jobs.

Sick and tired of that stupid problem and hungry to make a movie that might have just a little bit of the terrific success George Romero was having, I stayed up till the wee hours every night for about four weeks straight, writing my first full-length movie script, entitled *Intensive Scare,* and featuring what turned out to be my franchise horror character, Wayne Calley, who was a virtual embodiment of every serial killer in the plague of actual serial killers rampaging in every dark corner of America.

The movie might not have been made if I hadn't married Danielle. She read the script and then showed it to her dad without telling me. I was shocked when he took Danielle and me to dinner at his luxurious country club and said he would put up the money for me to make my movie. "I want you to succeed and make my little girl happy," he said. "I spoiled her too much, and she's not used to struggling. She believes in you, and I hope she's right."

I didn't know what to say. Saying that she *was* suitable would have been so outright ballsy it would have turned Jim Stanwix off. He said, "As you know, Ketchum has that chain of theaters as one of our big clients. You and Rocco met the owner, Clyde Goldberg when you were making his trailers. I want to agent your movie. If nothing else, I can get Clyde to run it in his chain."

This excited me no end because I had learned that getting a movie distributed was usually much more complicated than getting it made.

"That'd be great," I said, somewhat in awe.

He said, "Let's put our cards on the table. Danielle spilled the beans; I know you're secretly engaged. I don't want it to be a secret. First, let's have the wedding right out in the open. A big shindig, like she deserves. Then we'll get started making your movie. Maybe we can show the world that George Romero isn't the only talented guy in Pittsburgh."

"I'll drink to that!" Danielle said.

CHAPTER 14

I quit my ad-agency job in 1971, a few weeks after Danielle and I got married, and then I worked my butt off on my movie, wondering at times if it was doomed to fail ingloriously, like my dream of digging a pirate cave in my backyard. I offered Jimmy Costello a job on the production, but he turned me down, saying, "You and George Romero both can shove your crappy little horror flicks up your ass." I stopped reaching out to him after that. I decided that his envy and negativity were too toxic. I couldn't afford to let it drag me down.

All through the grind of the shooting schedule, I held my breath when the "rushes" came back from the lab -- but they kept looking as good as I had hoped, even though I had to fight down occasional worries that I was kidding myself. I continued to wrestle with self-doubts every step of the way. Still, when *Intensive Scare* opened on over a hundred screens, the kids who buy eighty-five percent of movie tickets flocked to the theaters despite several disparaging or downright vicious reviews. I had a hit on my hands, and theaters nationwide clamored to book it. I felt that Jim Stanwix's faith in me had been vindicated. And I loved Danielle even more for making it happen.

Flushed with that kind of success, I did not foresee the collapse of our marriage. It happened by slow degrees, instigated by financial disappointment and then disaster. Danielle's father had put up $500,000 for me to make the movie, which he had raised by selling off some blue-chip stocks in his portfolio. He had insisted on being in control of the finances till he got a total return on his initial investment, but as month after month crept by, that return wasn't happening. The theater chain owned by his buddy was reneging on our royalties, and to mitigate his losses, he was keeping a tight fist on the box-office returns from all the other chains, who were also short-changing us and over-charging for our share of cooperative advertising in all the markets.

Jim Stanwix was doling out little bits of money to me occasionally, making me beg for it and racking up every penny as advances against my illusive royalties. At the same time, he was lavishing money and gifts on Danielle because she was his daughter, and I was only a son-in-law. He blamed me for "dragging him into the movie business." He lost sight of the fact that he had decided to finance my movie of his own free will, and he was the one who had made the deals with the theaters that were ripping us off. Meanwhile, his financial situation had worsened because, in the first flush of glee over glowing box-office reports, he had sold even more of his portfolio so we could start making a sequel. But he lost faith in it even before I started shooting it. He started saying that I had married his daughter so I could play him for a sucker.

Worse, Danielle began to believe him. In 1972, while we still seemed like a couple with a rosy future, she gave birth to our daughter, Joy, and three years later, while I was making *Intensive Scare Part Two*, she divorced me. Her father shut the movie down, forcing me to file for bankruptcy, then used his high-priced lawyers to show the court that I lacked the means to give a three-year-old the financial support she required. The court awarded custody to Danielle, and I only had visitation rights.

While going through all this, I lived in a shabby apartment in a low-rent district on Pittsburgh's South Side, which had yet to be gentrified. The ugly storefront where New American Films had begun was still there. It was a downtrodden, crime-ridden neighborhood where I didn't want to bring my daughter on the rare days when I got to see her, so I usually brought her to playgrounds, movies, or places like Chuck-E-Cheese. I wanted to weep each time she hit me with a sad, puzzled look and asked me when I was coming back to live with her mommy.

I had to return to making TV spots, sales films, and political documentaries, this time not at Ketchum but on my own. It took me five years to get back on my feet. Eventually, a couple of my commercial clients, who loved my work and had a yen to be in the entertainment business, offered to put up enough dough to partner with me in a new production company. They filed a battery of lawsuits against the nest of thieves, including Jim Stanwix. Instead of delinquent royalties, I obtained all the rights to *Intensive Scare Part One* plus the raw footage on *Intensive Scare Part Two*. Then, they negotiated a new distribution deal on the proven picture and the one in the works, with a big chunk of front money that made me solvent again at age forty-one.

Back when I was broke, my notoriety as the creator of Wayne Calley seemed to mock me. Still, my pride was restored, as was my self-confidence as a filmmaker and as the father of a bright, beautiful now eight-year-old daughter who constantly reminded me of her mother and made me nostalgic for what might have been. I often remembered how Danielle and I would stand over Joy's crib when she was newly born, with our arms around each other, basking in the love we both felt for the beautiful little person we had created, and I never could figure out why so much in life had to go wrong.

CHAPTER 15

In August of 1980, twenty-eight years after the murders of my childhood friends, I was deep into the renewed shooting schedule on *Intensive Scare Part Two* when Biff Conley, Mo Brubaker, and Howie Drummond were released from prison. They were outfitted with ankle monitors while they awaited a new trial, which to me was an outright travesty. Vito Martinelli had left the Clairton police force and was now an investigator for the defense attorneys. I thought this move was traitorous because it might set the convicted murderers free. Biff's death sentence at the end of the first trial had already been commuted to forty years in prison, the same punishment levied upon his two accomplices, and now I feared that a new trial might set all of them free.

I had hired Vito as a technical consultant on my sequel to *Intensive Scare.* He took me aside on location while the crew was setting up for a shot and divulged his newly contrived connection to the case. He said he was letting me know about it in the interest of full disclosure because he was afraid I would not want him to work with him if I found out in some other way.

Angrily I said, "Well, it's still almost as if you were doing it behind my back because you know damned well that I had a personal connection to their victims."

"Please understand," he said, unperturbed, "that I may have found some exculpating evidence. Otherwise, I'd be glad to let them rot behind bars. I need to make sure they deserve what they're getting. That's what true justice is all about."

He was tight-mouthed about what his new evidence was. He understood I had remained convinced for almost three decades that Biff, Howie, and Mo were guilty, so he felt obliged to cushion the blow before I found out they would be released. He said he still wanted to remain my friend and didn't want me to hate him for his role in getting them out.

We met in his office in downtown Clairton. It was in a brand-new single-story brick building with dark wood trim that housed the law offices of the legal team that represented the freed defendants. It was one of the most attractive architectural layouts in town, made of pastel bricks and dark wood trim. The foyer had lush green carpeting and majestic potted plants under a tinted skylight. It was located near the new Ravensburg Bridge, the best way to enter town. If you came in from the lower approach, where the blast furnaces were, you would be greeted with roiling black smoke and a chemical shower that speckled your windshield with white specks. But if you entered from up on the hill, where the main business section was, everything appeared pleasantly copacetic, and you didn't usually have to think about the cancer-causing chemicals.

I drove the eight miles to Clairton from the upscale community of Pleasant Hills, where I had lived since my divorce. I wore jeans, sneakers, and a blue short-sleeved golf shirt with a pocket for my pen and phone. Vito was dressed more flashily in a white silk shirt and black sharply creased slacks, as was his style; even during his time on the police force when he wasn't highly paid. He always wore several flashy rings and gold chains when he was out of uniform and might've been mistaken for somebody slicker and more prosperous than he was. These days, though, he is doing quite well financially.

The frosted glass on the door to his office said in embossed golden letters: *Victor Martin, Private Investigations*. I looked at him with raised eyebrows, and he said, "I wanted to look

Waspish in the Yellow Pages. There is no Victor Martin. The lawyers who own this building are Wasps, who pretend not to be prejudiced against other nationalities, but that's not true. That's why I'm gonna move out when my lease is up."

"Are you going to change your name legally?" I asked amusedly, mainly to take a shot at him.

"No, it would kill my dago parents. They'd probably disown me."

I chuckled and then said, "So Mr. Wasp, a prospective new client with a lot of money to spend, gets in touch with you by phone and then sees you in person, and what do you tell him when he sees that you don't look like a white Anglo-Saxon Protestant?"

"Same thing I just told you, and by then, he probably won't return. Or she. I do pretty well with the ladies."

I didn't doubt that. I had seen how some of my actresses and female production people immediately perked up in his presence. Also, for that matter, some of the gay men. He was still
single and as handsome and charismatic as ever.

He unlocked the office door, led the way in, and turned on the lights. It was spacious and well-decorated, with an orange carpet and modernistic paintings on three off-white walls. He had an excellent oak desk, a leather sofa, a wooden glass-topped coffee table, and a credenza behind his desk that displayed an array of wine and liquor bottles.

"I'm having chardonnay," he said. "Good for you?"

"That sounds great," I said and waited while he got crystal goblets out of the credenza and brought them to the coffee table with a bottle of good wine, along with napkins, coasters and a bowl of Planter's mixed nuts with a silver spoon in it. As he poured our wine, I said, "This is a great place for you to greet your Wasp clients."

"Especially the ladies," he said with a grin that was almost a wink. "Here's to you and your new movie."

"*Our* new movie," I said. "You're working on it, too, you know."

He said, "I'm glad you didn't throw me under the bus."

We sipped wine from crystal goblets, and I thought about how impressive this genteel environment and its accouterments would be for any ladies he might have brought here. I needed a set like this for a scene in my movie, and I intended to ask him about using it when our talk about the upcoming trial was over. I used a delicate silver spoon to scoop some nuts onto a napkin embossed with his initials. I was trying to be patient, but my curiosity was needling me.

Vito said, "Well, we might as well get right into it. I'll tell you how it went down; then, you can ask questions. I must say right up front that I'm convinced they did not do the murders."

He gave me a blow-by-blow that returned to the beginning of his original investigation in April 1952. He said this was necessary so I could understand everything in context. And while he was talking, he let me thumb through his Murder Book, a compilation of the case's history through police reports that were bolstered by clippings from newspapers and magazines, such as this early one that came from the *Pittsburgh Press*:

THREE BOYS FOUND MURDERED

On April 15, the Tuesday after Easter Sunday, the naked and mutilated bodies of three pre-adolescent boys, Ronald Demick, Mickey Jenkins, and Joey Angelo, were found floating in a muddy pond in a patch of woods in Clairton, Pennsylvania. A spokesman for the mayor's office said, "This is truly one of the most horrendous crimes ever to occur in Allegheny County." The boys were stripped nude and "hogtied" with their shoelaces, their right ankles tied to their right wrists behind their backs, and the same with their left wrists and ankles. Their clothing was found in the pond, and some twisted-around sticks had been thrust into the muddy bottom. The clothing was turned inside out. One pair of boy's underwear was found about twenty feet from the pond, and there appeared to be blood on it.

The boys' autopsies revealed that Ronald Demick and Mickey Jenkins died of "multiple injuries," while Joey Angelo died of "multiple injuries with drowning." Joey had lacerations to various parts of his body and mutilation of his scrotum and penis.

The first missing person's report was made by Joey's stepfather, Armand Angelo. Initial police searches were cursory because they believed that the boys were probably runaways who would shortly return home, to the great relief of their parents. A more thorough search of fields and clearings behind some duplexes behind Farnsworth Avenue in Clairton was conducted by the Allegheny Search and Rescue Team supervising friends, parents, and volunteers proceeding shoulder-to-shoulder, but they found no sign of the missing boys.

A Farnsworth Avenue resident, Theresa Corrado, owner of a mom-and-pop store in the alley behind the duplexes, reported that she had seen the three missing boys heading into the nearby woods and had later seen Joey's stepfather shuffling down the alley, calling out for the young boy to come home. That led two patrolmen to go down the path into the woods, where they entered a log shack said to have been built by the boys and their friends, which is where they found a second pair of bloody underwear. They followed a blood-spattered trail, and further on was the pond where they came upon the boys' bodies.

Detective Vito Martinelli of the Clairton Police, who is heading the murder investigation, stated that he is hopeful that the clues found so far will lead to a speedy arrest because a crime This degree of depravity is usually not the last one of its kind that will be committed by the perpetrator if he is not swiftly apprehended.

I leafed through twenty or thirty pages of the Murder Book before I came upon crime-scene photos that I couldn't bear to look at. So, I averted my eyes, shut the book, and said to Vito, "Okay, I'm now as thoroughly immersed in ugly memories as I need to be, so what can you tell me as to why you think the bastards didn't do it?"

He said, "You were too young to be at the trial, and as you recall, we didn't feel that we needed your testimony about the bullying."

"No doubt you didn't need it," I said. "Because you got them convicted. And I was glad about it. So now you're gonna tell me I need to change my mind? Forgive me if I won't be easily moved in that direction."

"I think the new evidence will persuade you."

"Can I have some more of your excellent chardonnay? To fortify myself against whatever you're going to tell me."

"Help yourself. There's more in the credenza."

As I poured and sipped, he filled me in on things brought forward at the trial, some of which I had read about at the time and some of which I was not privy to.

He said, "At first, we suspected that at least one of the boys had been sodomized because traces of semen were on a pair of the underpants that were found at the crime scene. But whose semen? Perhaps the boys? Through masturbation? And the prosecution believed that a knife attack caused Joey's wounds, but a defense expert testified that they were most likely a result of animal predation."

"What *kind* of predatory animal? You don't think we have saber-toothed tigers in those woods?" I said with amused mockery.

"Turtles," Vito squelched. "Turtles live in that muddy pond. And when they get a chance, they go after the soft parts of a dead animal of any kind, even a human. No appendage's softer than a boy's testicles."

"Oh, shit!" I exclaimed. "I wish you hadn't said that." My appendage had faded at the mere thought of it.

"Well, when I was on the police force, I had to attend plenty of crime victims' autopsies, and it was an aspect of the job that I hated. But I had to do it to get a handle on the kind of killer.

I was looking for. "He paused and poured himself a second goblet of chardonnay. Then he said, "There were strands of human hair that Joey Angelo was still clutching in his right hand. He didn't let go of it even after his wrists and ankles were tied behind his back. An expert on hair evidence testified for the prosecution that the hair matched samples taken from Mo   Brubaker's   scalp.

But hair evidence isn't as great as TV shows portray it to be, not unless DNA can be extracted from a root, but that wasn't in the cards back then. Also, though, there was bite evidence. The prosecution presented expert testimony that bite marks on Joey's right forearm matched dental impressions taken from Maurice Brubaker."

"Well, it's better than hair evidence," I said. "It added up to a convincing guilty verdict back then, and to my mind, it still does. Vito, you haven't said anything that changes my mind."

He grimaced at me, showing a degree of impatience that he hadn't shown up till now.

He said, "Listen, Dave, the new evidence doesn't have to be definitive; it only has to shake up a judge enough to finally grant the new trial they've been after for all this time. How would you like to be penned up for twenty-eight years for something you didn't do?"

"I wouldn't like it for me or them if it were true. But since I think they did it, I don't care if they rot in hell. It's what I wish for them."

"Well, let me tell you a few things. Okay?"

"Yeah, please go on," I said with barely hidden disbelief that we were even having this conversation.

He said, "To sum up my arguments, people think hair evidence is a perfect way to nail a suspect, but the fact is that it is not. Dozens of prisoners have been freed when expert testimony

on so-called evidence of matching hair samples has been refuted. Charlatans have gotten rich going around this country, testifying trial after trial for big bucks. But nowadays, it's been shown to be fake science, and no reputable attorney will use it, I mean either defense attorneys or prosecuting attorneys."

"I already told you I'm well aware of that."

"I'm not trying to insult you. I know you're no dummy, and you always do a lot of research to make your movies more authentic."

"I try."

Vito went on. "The so-called bite mark on Joey's arm is about as worthless as the hair evidence."

"Oh, c'mon, why?" I challenged.

"Going back to the trial," Vito said, "a board-certified medical examiner never looked at the supposed bite mark. The defense's expert testified to that. Even the expert put on standby, the prosecution was forced to admit that the mark in question either was not an adult bite mark or that it might not be a bite mark at all -- it wasn't a clear enough impression. Furthermore, to bring us up to date on this factor, at the motion for a new trial two weeks ago, a new expert testified that even if it *was* a bite mark, it lacked sufficient definition to be matched to *any* of the defendants."

"Okay," I said. "I grant that those are some good points. But even so, they don't prove innocence. All they do is raise doubt."

This brought forth Vito's ironic smile. And he hit me with: "Reasonable doubt is the defense attorney's Holy Grail. You know that, David. It's why the new trial was granted." With that, I swallowed the dregs of my wine while I tried to swallow that there would be a new trial.

I couldn't counteract all of Vito's arguments. And I could see why the judges who heard the petition could not refute it. I had to admit they had done the right thing. But even so, I still hoped that Biff and his buddies wouldn't get off. I tried to figure out if this was because I remained convinced that they had killed my friends. Or if I was clinging to hatred against them that went back to the days of those pink bellies.

Pondering all this with heightened anguish as I drove home, I realized I had forgotten to ask Vito if I could use his office for an upcoming film location. I reminded myself to phone him in the morning. This was in the days before cell phones so that I couldn't do it on my way home.

CHAPTER 16

Six months later, in February 1981, the new trial began while I was in post-production with *Intensive Scare Part Two*. Over five weeks, while the defense and prosecution dodged back and forth, I read about it or watched reports on TV whenever I could. Vito regularly filled me in on pertinent details.

One day, during our editing, a funny incident happened. My go-to editor, Paul Logan, and I were working in an editing suite in a Pittsburgh professional building, and next door to it was a dentist's office. The door to the suite had an electric eye to warn us if anybody came sneaking around during the early hours when most of the other offices weren't open for business yet. Paul and I were trying to decide where to put an edit in an action sequence where a young male victim gets stomped on and kicked in the crotch by a brutal killer. We were playing a sound take over and over on the Moviola, and the actor's horrendous screams were resounding in the editing suite -- and the electric eye dinged. I rolled back in my chair and peered out into the hall, and an elderly gentleman in a suit and tie peeked around the corner with a frightened look on his face. And finally, he asked, quite shakily, "Are you...I mean...are you...uh...the dentist?"

Paul and I laughed, and I told him, "No, sorry, we're editing a horror film."

He backed out of the hallway, still looking shaky. This still ranks as one of the funniest things that ever happened while I was editing a movie, and sometimes, I tell it on stage and make the fans laugh when I'm a guest at movie conventions.

Paul and I were still chuckling about the incident when Vito Martinelli barged into the editing suite and said, "You won't believe this, David. Remember Biff Conley's girlfriend from way back when—Mary Ann Sumpter?"

I said, "Damn, Vito! This better be good! We're stuck on how to fix a blown shot."

He ignored me and just repeated, "Mary Ann Sumpter? You recall her?"

"Yeah, I remember her. So what?"

"It's not a *so what*. She recanted."

"Huh? Don't tell me."

"Yeah, I'm tellin' you. She phoned the defense attorneys I work for and came in and recanted. Mary Ann Sumpter. She's gotten her life in order; she even looks reasonably attractive these days, without the pimples and blackheads. She's married and has three kids. She works as a nurses' aide. She feels guilty for lying at the trial."

Without even turning away from the editing console, I said, "So, was she lying then, or is she lying now? I assume you tried to figure that out, Vito."

"We did. We administered a polygraph test right down the hall in the conference room.

Not only did she take it, but she was also anxious to. And she passed with flying colors. At the original trial, she claimed she was with Biff in the shack that you boys built during the time frame of the murders. Now she said it didn't happen."

I grimaced and shook my head. "It doesn't seem like a big deal," I told Vito.

He said, "I agree. But back then, she also told more elaborate lies. She claimed that in the aftermath of the murders, she went with all three defendants to a Wiccan meeting in an abandoned church in McKeesport, and they were all drunk and stoned on marijuana. We checked, and the church existed, just like she said, and those crazy kinds of meetings had been held there. She told us that at this meeting, the defendants bragged about killing the three boys as a sacrifice to Satan. So, we got her to wear a wire and try to get Biff to say as much on tape. But he skirted the subject and never confirmed that the Wiccan meeting ever happened. The prosecutors figured at the time that they would go to trial without it."

"You haven't told me anything concrete so far," I said. "Just loose ends that occur in just about every murder case, even when the defendant is guilty."

"I disagree," Vito said. "With Mary Ann recanting and with all the other stuff I told you about, I think it amounts to a shitload of reasonable doubt."

He turned out to be correct. The original verdict was overturned, and the new jury found the defendants not guilty.

That was it. They were free. And they couldn't be retried. And the prosecutors couldn't do a damn thing about it.

CHAPTER 17

I still visited my parents often, usually on Sundays. Over the years, they had mellowed out some, and frequently, they didn't fight while I was there. This was especially true when I had Joy with me, so I brought her whenever possible.

On a Sunday, after the editing and mixing of *Intensive Scare Part Two* were completed and the elements were at the lab where the first finished print would be pulled, Joy and I went to my parent's house for dinner. She was nine years old, quite pretty and intelligent, her pale blonde hair in twin ponytails tied with pink ribbons. My parents loved her and were on their best behavior around her. There was always tension between them, just under the surface, but still, they were on their best behavior, and I always appreciated those interludes.

Joy and I sat with them at their kitchen table. They asked Danielle how she was doing because they still cared about her, too, and were devastated when we got divorced.

"I don't like my stepdaddy," Joy yelled.

"Well, you have to try your best to get along with him, honey," my mother said mildly, habitually diplomatically. I often thought she was too mild, diplomatic, or forgiving. She cottoned to most people with persistent affability, believing that everybody had some good in them, while I felt some people weren't worth the powder to blow them up.

And I was not too fond of Danielle's new husband either. My opinion of Jeff Blaney was that he was a pompous ass, much like her overbearing father. Blaney thought he was too cool for words. This always reminded me of something Vito had once said: "There are two kinds of people in the world, slick and smart, and you don't have to be smart to be slick."

At my mother and father's small kitchen table, she served us roast beef, mashed potatoes, and green beans. She was an excellent cook—not a gourmet cook, but absolutely wonderful when it came to good old home-style staples. And she loved doing it, especially for family. On Sundays, ever since I was a little kid, she usually made one of her four specialty meals: roast beef, roast chicken with stuffing, chuck roast with roasted potatoes, or spaghetti and meatballs.

Looking at me appraisingly, she said, "Your hair is too long, David."

It was true that I hadn't been to a barber for five or six weeks, but long hair was a thing now, and my dad hated it.

He said, "You look like a goddamn hippie."

I just kept slicing and chewing without talking back to him. He had voted for Nixon twice and would have done it four more times, were it possible. He couldn't stand the war protesters and had said many times that they should all be deported or shot.

To my mother, I said, "I just finished a long stint in an editing suite, and I tend to bury myself in the task, to the exclusion of things like eating regularly or getting haircuts."

"Well, you look so handsome when you properly care for your grooming," she told me. "Are you ever intending to get married again? I wish you would, David."

"Who knows?" I said. "I'm not ruling it out, Mother."

"Are you going with anyone?"

"Diane Di Marco," Joy interjected with a sweet smile of approval.

"Oh! Isn't she...?" my mother began.

"Danielle's bridesmaid," I supplied. "One of them. The pretty brunette. We've been dating for a while now. I hired her as a production assistant."

"I like her," Joy said.

I didn't want my mother to ask probing questions, but my father cut that possibility short by saying, with an angry snarl, "I saw that murdering bastard Biff Conley in the Village Inn the other day. He was with his no-good father, and they were both drunk."

This jarred me not only with the revelation that Biff was hovering in the neighborhood but also with the memory of getting beat up by his dad and his dad's buddy.

"Sonofabitch should a been electrocuted," my father said.

"Watch your language, Johnny," my mother said mildly, meaningfully looking toward Joy.

Surprisingly, my father didn't snap back at her. Many times in the past, he would have slapped her or punched her for less. Of course, I wasn't a child anymore, so perhaps he realized I might deck him.

I offered to do the dishes when we finished the main meal, but my mother wouldn't hear of it. "I'm used to doing them," she said. "Go on; this is your day to relax."

To leave the house for a while, I told Joy, "Let's go for a little walk, honey."

We walked the upper half of Farnsworth Avenue toward a little playground that hadn't been there when I was a child. It was past the little store in the alley, which was still there. But the path behind the store, down through the orchard toward the shack we had built, looked inaccessible now. The hillside had been filled in with tons and tons of yellow clay, blocking the entrance to the path and expanding the area at the top of the hill to make more room for the little playground. It had a set of swings, a sliding board, and a seesaw, and that was about it, except for a picnic table and a couple of benches.

Joy and I have come here many times since she was three. Now, she was too big for the swings. We could've tried the seesaw, or she could've used the slide, but we weren't so interested in them.

From the edge of the clay hill, Joy peered down through the thick foliage and said, "Isn't that the place, way down there, where your friends were murdered?"

I wasn't even aware that she knew anything about it, so I didn't know what to say at first.

She saw my puzzlement and said, "I know all about it, Dad. Don't be so surprised. With the re-trial and all, it's been all over the news, you know."

"Yeah. When you were little, I never said anything about it. But now you can handle it. Right?"

"Mostly, I block it out. It seems strange that something so horrible happened to my father. But it didn't happen to me, so I can keep it at a distance."

"Someday, I'll tell you all about it—or as much as you want to know," I told her. We turned around and headed back to my parents' house, where my car was parked.

My mother didn't want us to leave yet. She stood on the porch to stop me from heading out without saying goodbye, which I wouldn't have done. She plied us with an offer of homemade apple pie and ice cream, and we gladly accepted.

It was about as good as any Sunday when I was with my parents. But I understand them better now than I used to. I had come to realize why my mother must have stuck with my father through all those beatings. Together, they had come through the Great Depression and sometimes argued over which one should get to eat a potato my father had swiped from their landlady's larder. It was a miracle and a blessing when he landed a good-paying job in the steel mill. Most of the other men in the mill towns had come through those same struggles and felt the same way. They had a quiet pride about them because they could provide for their families.

Most of the women were housewives and were content with that. They did the cooking, cleaning, and ironing and never complained about it. They were content with their lot in life, which was better than what they had before.

But if a wife was married to a man who beat her or emotionally abused her or both, she had just about no place to go. Most of them had few, if any, job skills. During World War II, many of them worked in factories and were vital to the war effort. But now the men were back and took the jobs back, too. Women with one or more children were in a hopeless situation. If they were brave enough to file for a divorce, they mostly had no way to earn a living that could support them and the children. So, they stuck it out and took the beatings. They hoped all the while that their husbands would change, but that seldom happened.

I lived in terror, along with my mother, all through my growing-up years. But I had come to realize that my life would probably have been worse if she had left my father. I would have grown up in poverty. I wouldn't have been able to go to college. And I wouldn't have the career that I have now.

Furthermore, my career and my fame had at long last made my father proud of me. He came to my movie premieres, along with my mother, and bragged about me in the mill and the saloons. He had been unable to take that kind of pride when I was a teacher, so he had denigrated me back then. Nowadays, he often complimented me for getting out of teaching, and I couldn't make him realize that I didn't do it because of any disrespect for the profession. I still respected it as much as I ever did, and I still had fond memories of some of my teachers. It was just that, for me, writing and filmmaking made me feel that I was competing in a big arena and satisfying the sense of adventure that always pulsed inside me.

But I didn't get enough years to enjoy the detente with my father. By now, his drinking had punished his liver so much that it was enlarged and filled with pus. Several times, he had fallen in the street, on the porch, or in the house, knocking himself out cold, and my mother had to call for ambulances. His doctor had warned him, "One of these days, John, if you don't stop boozing, you're going to fall down and never get up." My mother and I, and even Joy and Diane, had tried to get him to join AA, but he wouldn't listen. Each time he got back on his feet, he celebrated by getting drunk.

Finally, the doctor's prophecy came true. At age 76, he fell while getting out of his car in front of his little Farnsworth house, and he went into a coma. He lasted for five weeks in the hospital, but nothing much could be done for him. We were informed that his brain was no longer functioning. Yet, he looked as if sleeping peacefully, with a slight smile, as serene as a sleeping child. I knew the illusion wouldn't last, but my mother desperately wanted to believe he would recover again.

I went with her to the funeral home, and she selected one of the most expensive coffins. I thought she should've spent a bit less but didn't say so. Sensing my thoughts, she said, "He deserves it. He worked hard all his life." That much was true. He had never missed a day's work despite his drinking. I had thought that my mom would probably die first, and I was relieved that it didn't happen that way. She deserved to live out her "golden years" without suffering any more of his abuse.

At his funeral, Vito Martinelli told me, "You're in shock, even though you probably don't realize it. There was so much stress between you and your father that you couldn't feel anything yet. It takes about a month, then suddenly it will hit you full force."

One day, about four weeks later, I was looking at a photo portrait of my dad, taken in 1927. He was in a dapper three-piece suit, young and handsome and only twenty-one years old, brimming with youth and possibilities, his whole life stretching before him. I thought about how different it might have been if all the bad things never happened.

Suddenly, I was bawling like a baby and sobbing, "Daddy! Daddy! Daddy..."

Over and over, I cried out for him, with tears streaming down my face in the aching realization that the close relationship I had always desired with my father had no chance of ever happening.

CHAPTER 18

Intensive Scare Part Two had its world premiere in New York in 1983. Its distributor had kept it in the can for over a year due to a glut of slasher films; then it was timed for a Halloween release, a common strategy with horror movies. It opened on three thousand screens and grossed twice as much as the original movie. I spent six weeks doing all the morning shows and many other venues to maximize the publicity and box-office figures that my two partners loved. They were money people, not film people. In their exuberance over the take, they talked a lot about "striking while the iron is hot," meaning that we needed to land a multi-picture financing deal while our current release was "the greatest thing since sliced bread." They said we should hire a publicist to blow my horn for me, and the publicist should team up with my agents to broaden the effort.

Sam Raimi, one of the most successful directors in the world, with hits such as *The Evil Dead, Darkman,* and *Spiderman*, once told me that his first foreign rep, Irv Shapiro, president of Films Around the World, Inc., once imbued him with grandfatherly advice about agents. "An agent doesn't want to be your partner, he doesn't want to be your friend, he doesn't want to have a beer with you, he doesn't want to hear about your problems. All he wants to do is make money off you. If you stop making money for him, he'll drop you like a hot potato."

Having taken this lesson to heart, I always tried to help my movies make money. Unlike some of the more pretentious patrons of the movie business, I willingly complied with all opportunities to take on publicity gigs. This time, it was more of a strain than usual because I had separated from my fiancé. Diane Di Marco and I had gotten engaged during the shooting of the *Intensive Scare* sequel. I did the six-week publicity tour without her since the studio that distributed the movie wouldn't pay her to travel with me.

When the tour ended, we flew to Las Vegas and married. I felt that, at last, I had found my soul mate. We were as compatible as any show-biz couple, and she was supportive. I was looking forward to a time when Diane and I could relax and be together, and we decided that our honeymoon would be a short trip to Rome. Neither of us had ever been there.

Ten years ago, I booked a tour of Italy and several other foreign countries, but I had to cancel because my publisher begged me to stay and promote a novel. It was my first published book, and I was very pleased and excited about it. It was a novelization of *Intensive Scare*. The movie's success paved the way for my original goal of becoming a novelist. It was a two-dimensional novel, but it sold well. I could do more serious literary work, but I was imbued with a desire to write something big and important, maybe even a well-reviewed best seller. I viewed every life experience as a potential for broadening my perspectives and honing my talent, and I viewed going to Italy through that same lens. Diane and I were proud of our Italian heritage. Ancient Rome was once the capital of the known world, and we were both anxious to see it. She knew as well as I did that America's Founding Fathers had used their deep knowledge of Greek and Roman history to help them give birth to our democratic republic.

We had already taken Joy on tours of many historical sites in and around Pittsburgh, such as Fort Necessity, where George Washington had surrendered after his first battle of the French and Indian War; the reconstruction of Fort Ligonier, which was the outpost from which General Grant's troops had marched to launch their fatal attack on Fort Duquesne; the Clay Frick house and museum, together with his beehive ovens which were his early method of making steel; and much, much more, because Western Pennsylvania was an area of intense importance during our colonial period. We wanted to take Joy with us to Italy, but Danielle wouldn't consent, which pissed me off and greatly disappointed my daughter.

On a Sunday in April 1984, six days before Diane and I were to leave, we went to my mom and dad's place to say goodbye and took Joy with us. Dinner was roasted chicken with stuffing, mashed potatoes and gravy, corn on the cob, and Caesar salad, which I remarked was very apropos because it bore the name of the assassinated ruler. My mother said, "David, I didn't even think of that!" And she giggled girlishly. After dessert (butterscotch pie was my favorite as a kid), Diane helped my mother with the dishes while I worked on the Sunday crossword puzzle, and my dad buried himself in the newspaper. Then Diane and Joy walked up to the small playground, giving me time to watch the Steelers on wide-screen TV at the Village Inn.

The bar was noisy and crowded, but my old friends were absent. Most were married and had moved away to raise their own families. I sat on a stool between two strangers and ordered a draft beer, and the price had gone up from ten cents to half a buck. Still cheap. In downtown Pittsburgh, it would cost a buck and a half.

Somebody yelled, "*Gotcha*, son! Pay up! You owe me *two* shots! Two shots of the Lord and make it snappy!" I knew he wasn't talking about the Lord Jesus Christ but about Lord Calvert, the whisky.

Bang! He ricocheted a shuffleboard puck off the side of the board.

He had drawn my attention, and I recognized him as Biff Conley's father -- the same guy who had knocked me down and stomped on my kidneys back when I had agreed to testify at his son's plea for a new trial.

Then, the younger guy he was playing shuffleboard with turned around to go to the bar, and I recognized Biff himself.

His eyes met mine and bored into me.

I tried hard not to flinch. Then he averted his eyes and ordered the shots of Lord Calvert that his dad had just won.

The two re-took their bar stools, and old man Conley glowered at me.

In a bit of a while, Biff strode toward me, around the corner of the bar. I braced for a sucker punch. His hand came toward me.

"No hard feelings," he said. "You thought I killed your friends, so you tried to stop me from getting out of prison. I would've done the same thing in your place."

His right hand hung in front of me, and finally, I reached out and shook it. His grip wasn't firm, and my handshake at that moment was just as weak and uncertain.

He said, "I was a mean kid. I was raised that way. My dad was a marine."

Then he turned and rejoined his father, who was still glowering.

I was quite shaken and didn't quite know what to think. Had I misjudged Biff all these years? Had he been guilty of my friends' murders or not? If guilty, had he repented? If *not* guilty, had he mellowed out?

I didn't stay to watch the rest of the Steelers game. I drove back to my parents' house, just two blocks away. On the way, I phoned Vito and told him about Biff's quasi-apology.

"I suppose he means it," Vito said. "Looks like you have one less enemy, and that's not bad."

"I think he means it," I said.

104

"Not a bad note to start your trip to Italy on. Give me a call when you get back."

I smiled and promised to do that.

CHAPTER 19

In an episode of the TV series Iconoclasts, George Romero said, "When you decide that you want to become a filmmaker, you don't say you want only to be a horror filmmaker; you want to make films, period."

That was my attitude also, and when Diane and I got back from Italy, I was imbued with a desire to take my career in a direction apart from where my notoriety lay, which, of course, was with the raw, brutal thrills of the slasher genre. After being dwarfed by the Roman ruins and other artifacts of great accomplishment, I wanted to create something more profound and perhaps more lasting than I had done before. I was aware that this desire might be vainglorious. I read an essay by Mark Twain on how to create lasting fiction, and after laying out all his points paragraph after paragraph, he said: "Now, if you do all *that*, you may be able to produce something that lasts forever. By *forever,* I mean thirty years."

Thus chastened, I embarked on the most ambitious work of fiction I had ever attempted, a big, ambitious novel that would cover four decades of American history as seen through the eyes of five iconic Americans. A comment from Tom Brokaw partly inspired it: "We were in a different country after those shots rang out in Dallas." My book was to be entitled *Dealey Plaza*, and it would not be about the Kennedy Assassination per se but about how what happened there was a turning point for our nation. In my opening paragraph, I stated, "It was as if we came all unsuspecting to a fork in the road and got shoved by cataclysm onto a darker, more dangerous path."

I buried myself in research and began outlining and writing parts of that novel while taking a long break, a hiatus from movie making, for two years following the successful release of *Intensive Scare Part Two*. I was pulling in enough money that I didn't need to feel pressured to plug in movie projects, and my two partners were happy to take up the slack. They relished getting to hobnob with some of the "big names" of the biz, and they enjoyed being treated like power players.

My wife warned me that I wasn't paying enough attention to the company, but I was so lost in my novel that I didn't listen. To make a long story short, my partners got "drunk on the smell of their cork" -- another Mark Twain saying -- and committed far too much of our bankroll to unfavorable pickup deals on shaky co-productions. A "negative pickup deal" is one in which you finance a movie in advance, and a bank commits to "making you well" once a distributor picks up the movie and makes a profit.

Unfortunately, the co-productions bombed. They never got "picked up." And so, after working for two years on my novel, it was still an unfinished work, and my film company was in deep trouble. So, I had to put the *Dealey Plaza* novel aside and find backing for another horror movie because that genre would be the most welcoming. At this point, I decided I was disillusioned with partners who could derail my career, even if they weren't intentionally trying to rip me off. They had just backed the wrong movies. Luckily, enough money was left for them to buy me out at a modest level, so I asked them to do it, and they complied. It gave me enough of a bankroll that Diane and I could go for roughly the next six months, able to pay our bills while I tried to get another big project going. I didn't want it to be *Intensive Scare Part Three*. I needed a break from Wayne Calley and all his gore and mayhem, which was starting to get to me, even though it was fake.

I caught a break while trying to figure out which direction to take. My literary agent phoned me from his New York agency and was pleased to inform me that, based on the success of my Intensive Scare novelization, he had landed me a three-book deal with Simon & Shuster. The advance was substantial and would help Diane and me get by for a year without tapping into the buy-out money from my former business partners.

The whole time that I was dealing with the ups and downs of my career, I had never stopped being tormented by the nagging knowledge that if Biff and his two buddies didn't kill my friends, somebody else must have. Maybe Biff was innocent, but the other two weren't. Perhaps somebody else entirely was the murderer. I didn't know.

About three months after I signed the contract on the three-book deal, Maurice Brubaker hanged himself in a jail cell in Clairton. Vito hit me with the news one day when we met at his office to go in one car to a good neighborhood bar called The Terrace Garden, where they had seventy-five-cent pizza slices on Tuesday nights. I rang the bell; he came out all set to go and said, "We might as well take your car since it's warmed up." This was in early December of 1989, and although no snow was predicted, the temperature was several degrees below freezing.

We hopped into my Buick, I re-started the heater, and he said, "Guess what, Dave? Maurice Brubaker hanged himself." That's the way he dumped it on me. Sometimes, he liked to try to shake me up. He had succeeded, and I didn't know what to say or how I should feel.

"He was picked up on a D&D," Vito continued. "He was going around getting in bar fights and making a nuisance of himself ever since he came here. One of the jailers found him with his T-shirt tied through the bars and wrapped around his neck. It looked like he was damned determined to die. His knees touched the concrete floor, so he could've stood up and saved himself if he wanted to."

I said, "Not if he was unconscious. He might've pulled himself up and let himself drop, which could've knocked him out."

"Yeah. Now, the money will only have to be split two ways. If they get any."

"What money?"

"Biff, Mo, and Howie had a joint lawsuit for wrongful imprisonment. My lawyer buddies don't think it'll fly, though. You never know what a jury will do, but like many people around here, they probably think those boys were guilty and got off on a technicality. So, they won't want to give them any money."

"Why would Mo hang himself if there were a chance he'd end up rich?" I asked Vito.

"I would guess that he couldn't handle freedom. It happens to a lot of ex-convicts. Not thinking about what to do with their lives becomes an ingrained habit. After they've been locked up for a couple of decades or more, not having to wonder what to do with themselves or how to earn a living or a million other things that most of us face every day, they'd rather be back in prison. Or dead. It seems crazy, but it's true."

After we were seated at the bar at The Terrace Garden and ordered our pizza slices, we started sipping our beers, and Vito said, "I wish I could think of some fresh evidence. The real killer needs to be strapped onto a gurney."

"I wonder if the crime scene was given a thorough search," I ventured to say. "In 1952, it was a foregone conclusion that Biff and the boys were guilty."

"Not right away, Dave. The public might've thought that, but the detective squad didn't. We didn't zero in on them until we pursued several other leads that didn't pan out. When the victims' bodies were found, not only the pond but also an area for as much as fifty yards all around got the same kind of meticulous attention as any other crime scene, even more so."

"But those woods were thick. Do you think anything could've been missed?"

"I was *on* that search, and I guarantee it was thorough."

"I don't doubt you," I said. "But still..."

We fell silent, sipped our beers, and I ordered another round. Our pizza slices had yet to arrive.

I didn't want the subject to drop, so I said, "It's a cold case, and Clairton is like any other small town. They don't have a cold case unit."

Vito surprised me by saying, "Just for the hell of it, would you want to go down there? We can have a look around. Back then, it was summertime, and the weeds were dense. Right now, the vegetation would be a lot sparser."

"Are you serious?"

"Yeah. I guess I am," he said.

The following Saturday was warm for December, crisp and sunny, not cold.

We couldn't take the path down to where the shack and the bull-rope swings used to be because the hill and the orchard had been filled with tons of yellow clay. So, we drove along the river along the river's bottom part of Clairton till we could enter the woods the back way. A gas company right-of-way, a broad dirt road, led into the woods a couple of miles below where the swings and the shack used to be. This was the route through which we had dragged the stolen bull ropes from the barges on the river up through the path in the woods to the clearing where we hung the ropes from the tree.

Amazingly, the little bridge across Peter's Creek was still there—or the half bridge- because it had no floor. When I was a kid, I usually had no money, so I couldn't pay a quarter to ride the bus to the swimming pool. There was yet to be a Ravensburg Bridge that could be walked across to get to the pool. And I wasn't allowed to hitchhike, although I sometimes did it anyway. The only other choice was to walk down the path through the orchard and past the swings to where the Peter's Creek Bridge was. Then, since the bridge floor no longer existed, I had to cross it by carefully walking its steel span and hanging onto the rafters. Then, up through the woods section leading to the swimming pool. By the time I got there, I was usually so sweaty and caked with sand from the last hill I had to climb that I could barely wait to plunge into the chlorinated water.

Vito Martinelli, who was ten years my senior, said he used to do the same thing when he was a kid. Lots of Clairton kids did. We laughed about it as we started eyeballing the wooded and stony ground. We picked up some long sticks to poke around with and moved ahead, keeping reasonably far apart, with a faint hope of spotting anything helpful. But it was a good day to be out in the woods, even if our mission was dubious.

After an hour or more, we were several hundred yards up the path that we both had traversed many times as kids and so far, our efforts have been fruitless.

I said, "I don't think kids still play in the woods nowadays. The path is almost totally grown over. I can barely make it out in places."

Vito said, "They don't play pickup games either like we used to. All they do is fiddle with their I-pads and their phones. None of them get any exercise. In not too many years from now, I figure muscles will be obsolete."

We didn't even chuckle at that. It was too sad, too much like a doomsday prediction. We kept moving up the path, each scanning the woods on either side, me on the left and Vito on the right.

About fifteen minutes passed, and then he said, "Hey, David, what do you think that is up there?"

111

He pointed upwards and to his right at an eroded hillside, but I couldn't tell what he meant initially.

"That smooth yellowish thing," he said, still pointing.

"Looks like the top of a stone to me," I said, finally making it out.

"Maybe not. Let's go and check."

We climbed up there, our shoes slipping in the eroded dirt, and Vito poked at the yellowish thing with his stick. Then he got on his knees and started scooping away dirt with both hands.

To my amazement, the thing had eye sockets. It was a human skull. Vito stood up, and we stared down at it. "We better leave it like it is," he said. "We've gotta get an anthropologist to unearth it the rest of the way. And probably a coroner. Maybe they have a way of figuring out who this was. And the cause of death."

I said, "They'll start by estimating the age and sex. Right?"

"Yeah, and how long it's been here. They'll do a painstaking excavation to see if there are more bones, either with the skull or nearby. Suppose scavengers have yet to carry them off. They'll search down this hill in case some of the bones might've been washed away by the kind of erosion that exposed the skull. It'll be helpful if they find the pelvis; that's the best indication for male or female."

My brain was already swimming with possibilities, and I said to Vito, "What if whoever this was killed by the same person who killed the three boys? We might have a serial killer on our hands, Vito."

He said, "One thing that has always puzzled me is why the killings stopped with the boys in the pond. Usually, that kind of sicko doesn't just stop."

"Well, maybe he didn't," I said grimly.

We both fell silent, mulling over the fact that we had known about three murders, and today, we may have unearthed evidence of a fourth one, long unknown.

Vito eyed me with an odd, raised eyebrow look on his face, but he didn't say anything. I didn't know what that look implied. But I was to find out by and by. And when I did, it put a rift in our friendship.

CHAPTER 20

After Vito and I found the skull in the woods, several months went by, and it still hadn't been identified. The day after our find, an anthropologist from Carnegie-Mellon University, Dr. James Kessler, had supervised a team of his students in painstakingly laying out grids and sifting dirt to find more human bones. Dr. Kessler was thrilled when they located the mandible. They also found ankle and foot bones and one ulna, the long, thick thigh bone. That was it; it could be assumed that animals had carried away the rest.

In 1989, the forensics associated with DNA analysis wasn't yet available to them. Vito tried to find a sketch artist or a computer artist who might be able to develop a likeness using the skull's features as a starting point, but the small Clairton police department wasn't about to spring for the kind of money it would have cost.

Dr. Kessler estimated the length of time that the owner of the skull had been dead and assigned it a likely span of roughly twenty to thirty years, which didn't pinpoint a workable time frame for any missing person that the police department knew about. No other bones were found either. Kessler thought the skull was male, but that wasn't a hard and fast opinion. He said that the facial features were delicate enough to be female but could also pertain to a small-boned male.

What it all boiled down to was that what Vito and I considered a startling discovery was getting us nowhere.

I did what I always did. I moved ahead with my career as best I could. By now, George Romero's Night of the Living

114

Dead and its many spinoffs and rip-offs have undeniably become a worldwide phenomenon. Inspired by that, I strove to make my unique entry into the zombie genre.

In late summer 1990, while writing a screenplay called *Daughters of the Dead*, I looked up from my desk and said to Diane, "This is going to make a fortune."

She said, "I hope you're right. But I think we don't need much money to be happy."

Like me, and unlike my first wife, Danielle Stanwix, Diane came from a low-income family that valued hard work, dependability, and honesty. Her father wasn't abusive like mine was, but when my father was sober, they got along quite well. They were both mill workers, but my father seethed with bitterness and disappointment, while Diane's father was content with his lot in life. He liked me, and I liked him. We laughed at each other's jokes. We drank the same beer brand and rooted for the Pirates and the Steelers. My mom and Diane's mom got along well, too. Maybe they both would've liked to have more children, but they weren't complaining. Diane was the only child in her family, and so was I, but we certainly hadn't been pampered. We didn't expect anything to be handed to us, and making money wasn't our be-all and end-all. True enough, making movies was expensive, and if my movies bombed, I would only be making them for a short time. But Diane and I both felt that we didn't need the so-called "glitz and glamour" of Hollywood. I had a movie agent in L.A. and a literary agent in New York City, but I said, "Let them sell the projects where the money is unreal, and I'll spend it here where it's real."

Our home in Pleasant Hills, eight miles from downtown, was upper-middle-class but not ritzy. It had a pleasant backyard and a nice in-ground pool, where I swam fifty breaststroke laps almost every day in the summertime after doing some calisthenics and light barbell and dumbbell work. I was content with being a suburbanite and keeping a low profile, so fans usually wouldn't intrude on me.

Pittsburgh has most of the things much bigger cities boast about -- a major symphony and ballet company; pro football, baseball, and hockey teams; earthy ethnic neighborhoods; world-class universities; stellar research institutes and museums -- yet it's small enough not to have a huge crime rate or massive traffic jams. It has almost every kind of film location that might be required. Some parts of it can double for a major city like New York, yet there are rural locales just twenty or thirty miles outside town.

I wrote *Daughters of the Dead* so it could be shot in Pittsburgh on a much lower budget than in most other places, especially Hollywood. I was excited about it because it was the unique take on the zombie genre I had been striving for. It was designed to take established zombie folklore in a whole new direction.

The main idea of the plot was that pregnant women were bitten by ghouls during an outbreak of the undead and were allowed to deliver their babies before the authorities shot them in the head and burned them in a bonfire. But nobody knew what these babies might turn into.

Would they always be as perfectly normal as they seemed to be? Or not? To try to find out, the government's nefarious plan was to set up communities run by the CIA where the babies would be raised by unsuspecting adoptive parents and secretly studied by doctors and scientists as they matured.

What could go wrong?

My gimmick was that the children would appear normal till they reached puberty. But then they would turn into vampires. And anybody bitten by them turned into a flesh-eating zombie. So, these "special children" with secret powers eventually would oversee a pack of undead flesh-eaters that would help them take over a small town...and perhaps the world.

I thought George Romero would want to team up with me to get this project made, so I gave him the script. He read it and liked it a lot, but by now, Russ Streiner, a highly skilled producer and filmmaker, had left to start his own production company, and George had some new partners who did not want to help me in any way. They considered me a competition. So, I had to raise the money to make the movie alone.

Meanwhile, I had to deliver the first novel in my three-book deal with Simon & Shuster. So, when I wasn't wheeling and dealing with potential movie investors and distributors, I was hard at work bashing out *The Majorettes*, a thriller about lovely teenage girls in the clutches of a serial killer -- but it wasn't just a series of brutal murders, I gave it a complex, suspenseful storyline and believable and sympathetic characters.

Even though I had to work hard at maintaining my career, I never forgot the fact that the murders of my boyhood friends would never have been solved if Biff, Mo, and Howie hadn't done it. Mo had taken himself out of the picture, and I tended to believe, on gut feelings, that Biff wasn't guilty. That left Howie Drummond. And if Biff wasn't guilty, Howie probably wasn't either.

Then, there was the skull that Vito and I had found in the woods. Was it related to the deaths of the three boys or not? So far, it hadn't been identified, and there didn't seem to be a chance that it would be.

Once again, the case had stagnated. But I couldn't get it out of my mind no matter how involved I was in more immediate things. I knew, from my extensive study of murder and its effect on victims' friends and families, that there was no such thing as "closure." At a young, impressionable age, my life had been shattered by the violent death of someone close to me, and I had never gotten over it. Nor did I want to. I couldn't bring myself to erase the event from my mind. To do so would have seemed an insult to Ron and Mickey's memories. I continued with my writing and filmmaking efforts, never feeling entirely free of the unfinished past. I don't mean that it consumed me with the force of an obsession, but I do suggest that it was always there, quietly lurking.

In September 1990, my daughter Joy was about to start her freshman year at the University of Pittsburgh, majoring in journalism, when she came to my house one night in tears and confided to Diane and me that she didn't want to live with her mother and stepfather anymore. Diane and I got her to settle down, gave her tea to sip, and told her that she was of age to make her own decisions but not to do anything hastily.

"You're eighteen now," I told her, "and if you want to stay in a dorm at Pitt, that will get you away from them for at least nine months while you figure things out. Would your mother go along with something like that?"

"Why can't I live with you?" she blurted, bursting into tears again.

I thought it over, feeling terrible.

Diane came to Joy and hugged her. Calmly and reassuringly, she said, "Don't worry about me. I'm okay with whatever the two of you decide."

I wouldn't have expected anything less from her, but it was still lovely to hear.

I said, "Joy, honey, your mother and I have always been on an uneasy truce where you're concerned, but if you tell her you don't want to live there, she might feel rejected and react very badly."

Joy hotly contradicted me. "Dad, she doesn't care what I do! She'll be relieved if I'm not her responsibility from now on! That way, she can travel from coast to coast with her rich husband and their snooty friends. They're sickening!"

"Would they still pay for your tuition at Pitt? Or not?"

"I don't know."

"Well, if they won't, I think I can manage it. But I don't have the kind of money that I used to have."

"I'll work in the student cafeteria if I have to!" Joy said vehemently.

She knew, as well as Diane and I did, that no student job would dent her tuition, but we didn't need to make that an issue right now. Instead, we got Joy into a calmer state of mind by telling her that I would speak with her mother and try to smooth a path forward that would allow her to move in with us with minimal animosity. I told Joy just to let me handle it and get started at Pitt without worrying herself to death.

As it turned out, Joy was correct about how her mother and stepfather would react. We got only token resistance -- a few obligatory questions and reservations -- about the proposed change in circumstances. And so, with great relief, Joy Diane and I gladly brought my daughter into our Pleasant Hills home. Jeff Blaney, Danielle's rich wheeler-dealer of a husband, salved their consciences by continuing to pay Joy's college tuition.

In the meantime, *Daughters of the Dead* was optioned quite a few times during Joy's freshman year, and I made a lot of money for doing nothing except granting the options, but the production money itself has yet to come through. Then, I got a chance to pitch the project to Joseph Stern, one of the financiers of Wes Craven's smash-hit *Nightmare on Elm Street*. I had been trying to secure three million dollars to make the movie, but Joe proposed that he fund it entirely out of his own line of credit. His idea was to make it on a low budget -- half a million- and together, we would make a fortune selling foreign rights worldwide. By keeping production costs low but still turning out to be a highly marketable product, we should rake in at least three million, maybe more, and split the profits fifty-fifty. For a while, it looked like my prediction that the project would make Diane and me a lot of money was about to come true.

But alas, it didn't turn out that way. As soon as Joe went to his bank and transferred the necessary money into a joint production account, it turned out that he wanted to produce his daughter's script, not mine. It was a cruel twist of fate that I certainly had not bargained for. But I didn't wish to waste the summer without making a movie, so I finally said that I would produce the film in Pittsburgh if Kari Stern would work with me to revise her script, which in its present form was, in my opinion, a guaranteed flop. I worked with her through five revisions, Finally, I told her and her father that it was good enough to shoot.

But as soon as the money was released, she returned to her original version and refused to change a single word, and her father let her get away with that.

By this time, I had enlisted some of the top people in the horror genre to come in and work with me on the movie at less than they usually would have been paid. They had all signed on because they thought in the beginning, as did I, that it would be *my* movie.

But not only was it *not* going to be my script, but Kari also hired a new director without consulting with me, and he was a total loser who didn't know his butt from a hole in the ground when it came to shooting a movie. This violated my agreement, but if I had resigned, all the highly talented people I had hired would have lost a summer's work. I couldn't do that to them and still retain my self-respect. So, I stuck with it through one of the most miserable periods of my career, including the six-week shooting schedule plus editing and post-production, all the way into the early winter of 1992.

On the plus side, my daughter got to work on the movie during the summer shooting schedule, which was good for her as a journalism major, and Diane got paid well as an assistant producer. I got paid an advance of $90,000 as the line producer, but nothing out of the back end because the picture was so crappy it didn't make a dime.

Ironically, the so-called "director," who was as responsible as anyone for how badly the movie turned out, trashed the hell out of me in *Hollywood Reporter* and said that the fact that *Daughters of the Dead* ever got made was "a prime example of everything that's wrong with Hollywood." He was blissfully unaware that he fit perfectly into that category.

CHAPTER 21

After the 'Daughters of the Dead' fiasco, Joy was back at Pitt, and Diane and I were trying to unwind from the assault on our sensibilities. I made the deadline for submitting the finished manuscript for *The Majorettes*. A funny little incident occurred while I was amidst a few revisions. Helga, the evil nurse in the story, had been left alive in the original manuscripts, and my editor at Simon & Shuster had suggested that she should die at the hands of the main villain. Diane and I had lunch at a family restaurant and were getting into my car when I said, "I have to go home and kill Helga." I heard a sharp intake of breath and turned to see an elderly woman staring at me, utterly shocked. I got in the car and shut the driver's door, leaving the passerby wondering if I was going home to kill a cat, a dog, or a person. Diane and I got a good laugh over it. I finished the Helga death scene and sent the revision to my editor, and a few days later, she called and told me how much she liked it. I told her about the woman who had overheard me planning Helga's murder, and she chuckled. I was relieved that the manuscript was accepted, and now I had to turn my attention to coming up with a marketable idea for the second novel of the three-book deal. But for now, the pressure was eased, and the final payment of my advance was on its way, and Diane and I could relax and unwind.

Ever since my dad died, we have been frequently picking my mother up and taking her to lunch or on shopping trips, things to brighten her days and prevent her from feeling too lonely. We had asked her to move in with us, but she did not want to "be a burden." We assured her we'd love to have her with us, but she still demurred.

But now we had started noticing that she wasn't bathing regularly and keeping herself as neat and proper as she had done all her life. It got so that when I phoned her to tell her we'd be arriving, I had to remind her to take a shower and be ready. She'd say, "I know, I already did that." But she hadn't. When she got in the car, she smelled terrible.

On days when Diane and I helped her bring some groceries in, the house also had an odor. The place was a mess, totally unkempt, with dirty dishes and greasy pots and pans piled into the sink and on the table, counter, and side cabinet. My wife and I put the groceries away, and she opened the cabinet under the sink to get soap and scouring pads to start washing and drying.

She said, "Oh, my, David! Look!"

Under the sink was a raw chicken that my mom had obviously intended to put into the refrigerator but had put into the sink cabinet instead. It didn't smell; it was sort of mummified. We took it out, put it into a plastic bag, and dumped it in the garbage.

Now, we knew that something severe was going on with my mother. She wouldn't enjoy her golden years as I had hoped. Instead, she was being taken down slowly but indeed, by Alzheimer's.

Over the next several years, Diane and I tried to do the best we could for my mother as her disease progressed with slow, painfully dismaying certainty, and she became more and more helpless and in need of the kind of care that we could not provide. We started by resorting to a personal care home but eventually had to take her to Kane Hospital in McKeesport. Her tenure there lasted for about a year and a half till she could no longer feed herself and had to be fed through a hole in her stomach.

123

Then, there came a day when I saw sores all over her arms and legs. I became angry, thinking that they were bed sores and that she wasn't being watched over and turned over in her bed. However, I was informed that they were the kind of sores that patients eventually developed when they became allergic to the highly nutritious manufactured food that was being fed through a stomach tube. Now, there was no alternative way to feed her, and she would slowly starve to death as all her bodily functions would shut down.

Up till then, I had thought that Alzheimer's disease only affected the mind but not the body. Now, I learned that the mind would lose control over a person's organs in its later stages. So, we had no choice but to stop giving my mom food and let her slowly starve to death. I had to meet with a panel of six doctors to permit them to remove the feeding tube.

One of the doctors said, very sympathetically, "She is not going to die quickly because the food she's been getting all these months is optimal nutrition. Be prepared for a lengthy vigil, Mr. Cristi."

It took her six weeks to die, and Diane and I were called in when it was close to the end. It was one of the worst things I had been through thus far in my life. She wants her suffering and misery to be over, yet she does not want to be without her.

All I could do was hold her hand while Diane held mine.

I had not told my daughter, Joy, because I didn't want her to have to be there. I had kept her away from most of the worst manifestations of my mother's illness. She was young and needed to enjoy her life while she could. I always believed that all of us should do that. Deal with life's sorrows when you must, and don't shirk them, but make the most of the good times with friends and family. Nobody escapes life unscathed, but we mustn't bask in its miseries.

CHAPTER 22

A week or so after my mother died, Vito came to visit Diane and me at our house in Pleasant Hills. He was with his new girlfriend, Donna Florian, and I grilled steaks on the patio. Joy was home, so she ate with us. Then we frolicked in the pool and batted a beach ball around for a while. Then Joy went to her room to study, and the rest of us talked, laughed, and drank too much wine.

Donna was twenty years younger than Vito -- the way he liked them -- and she got all bubbly and lovey-dovey, sitting in his lap and kissing and hugging him, and he got perturbed instead of pleased with her. They got into a spat. He told her to get away from him, settle down, and stop acting like a teeny bopper. I thought he was being boorish and unfair. Her teeny-bopper days were behind her, but she did have a long ash-blonde ponytail and a firm figure that belied her age.

She got up in a huff and went through the sliding glass door that led to the powder room. Diane said, "Vito, chill out. You go after the young stuff, but then you get mad when they act like it. At least Donna is your age, more than most of the others. You should be glad she likes you so much."

Diane was one of the few who could upbraid him like that and make him take it. He shook his head at his churlishness, and when Donna returned, he apologized. She bent down and kissed him on his forehead, then poured herself some more wine, but to show she wasn't back in his camp yet, she moved over to a separate lawn chair.

In a little while, still looking sheepish, he said, "Come on back, honey, I'll pull your chair over." She got up, and he did so. He smiled at her and said, "I love this woman. I think I'm gonna marry her."

"Only if I let you," she told him saucily.

"She's not only cute but spunky," he said with an abashed smile.

He liked younger women for their vivacity, spontaneity, and, for them, tight, youthful bodies, but he was annoyed when, at times, they'd rather not be as severe as he was about certain things. I was glad I was in love with Diane, who was close to my age and whose insights were sharper than mine in quite a few ways. She was as vivacious as I wanted her to be. I deeply valued her and wanted to keep it that way; in other words, I wanted our marriage to last. And now that we had Joy with us, there was even more reason to feel that way.

I told Vito, Donna, and Diane about an amusing conversation with a young barmaid at a movie convention when I was out of town. Obliquely, what I had to say was aimed at Vito, but I thought I could disguise that fact by telling all three of them about it, especially now that we were tipsy. "To be honest," I said, "this girl was beautiful, bright, and articulate, like Joy. I tried to set her at ease by saying, don't worry, I enjoy talking with you, but I'm not going to hit on you. I'm way too old for you. *All* men are attracted to young girls, but some of us have *sense.*"

"You better have," Diane said. But she trusted me. I think.

"I'm plenty young enough for *this* guy!" Donna said. "At least I better be."

Vito smiled but said nothing.

To change the subject, I told them the basic plot I had in mind for my next novel to see what they thought about it. One of my favorite themes has always been technology gone awry. I always looked for new developments that might lend

126

themselves to fiction with a horrific slant. I had read an article in *Newsweek* about electrodes that had been implanted in the brains of epileptics to control their seizures. By probing with the electrodes, scientists mapped all the regions of the human brain and discovered, to their amazement, that they had found a way to stimulate and control various emotions and behaviors as they might wish.

"Dig this," I said. "A professor at Yale is advocating that all human beings should be implanted with electrodes at birth to create a more peaceful and productive society. What if all the kids at an exclusive preschool in Manhattan were being secretly controlled and manipulated by scientists in cahoots with the government? That's the basis for my new novel, *Day Care*. I think of it as Rosemary's Baby of Technology."

"I *like* it, honey!" Diane said.

"Me, too," said Donna. "Could you turn it into a movie?"

"If someone would finance it," I said wryly. "I can make any movie for which somebody will put up the money."

Vito held back and did not comment. But later, when the two women entered the house to prepare dessert, he said to me, "Hey, buddy, I'm not dumb. Your little story about the barmaid was aimed at me."

I thought I should find a way to apologize.

But he said, "Don't worry, I'm not mad. I might surprise you by taking it to heart."

I wished he would, but I doubted it.

CHAPTER 23

The milestones of life keep coming no matter what. There's a saying: Men plan, and God laughs. I had seldom seen Jimmy Costello in recent years. I had tried to stay in touch, but he hadn't. I didn't know much about his circumstances, and I had no idea he was in bad health, especially at such a young age. I still hope that we will renew our old friendship and camaraderie. It was a shock to me when he died in the summer of 1992, a month and a half before Vito Martinelli's wedding.

He was only 53 years old, and he died of cirrhosis of the liver. By this time, he had pulled away from all of us who used to be his closest friends and had descended into alcoholism, self-pity, and malignant bitterness. He and our old comrade, Brent Julian, from the days of New American Films, had visited me for three days on location during the shooting of *Daughters of the Dead,* and every evening, we dined at an excellent Italian restaurant, got loaded, and shared a million laughs. I told them about the piece of crap I was stuck making, and Jimmy pretended to commiserate, except I thought he was faking it. Underneath his smiles and his laughs, I think he was glad about what a flop my new picture would probably be.

At the funeral home, his long-suffering and in-denial wife, Jeannie, was still in thrall to his idealized memory. He had been cremated, the ornate silver urn was there on a pedestal, and she had brought a DVD of a half dozen 8-millimeter films he had made over the years, apparently not with an intent to market them, but only to show off his talent to friends and family and bask in their praise. We mourners sat there and watched his little films, and I felt sad that he had never realized his potential due to his own bitterness. It also occurred to me, with considerable ruefulness, that Jimmy Costello had lived a reasonably long life while sabotaging himself. At the same time, Ron Demick, Mickey Jenkins, and Joey Angelo never got that chance. But I was learning, as people all around me left this world no matter how old they were, that if life was about anything, it was about loss. And about making the very best we could out of it while it lasted.

I was surprised when Vito Martinelli sprung on me at the funeral home that he and Donna Florian would get married. I knew he was now 63 because he was ten years my senior. Donna was around 53, but I didn't ask him. She could pass for 35 or 38, the age bracket he usually hits on nowadays. True enough, he could still pass for around 50 and acted as if he were much younger. He said, "I'm done tomcatting around. Gotta settle down sometime, and it might as well be now."

His wedding took place at his house in an upscale neighborhood of Clairton called Bickerton Estates. He had bought the place two years after he left the police force to become a well-paid private investigator. If it had been in ritzy Mt. Lebanon, it would have been valued at half a million, but since it was in Clairton, he could snag it for only $90,000. It was a four-bedroom brick ranch with a sprawling, well-landscaped lawn, an in-ground pool, and a four-car garage.

There were about twenty guests at the informal reception, including the priest, the mayor, and the chief of police. Joy stayed until the bride was kissed a short while longer, then met some college friends at a mall. After she departed, several people mentioned how pretty, articulate, and funny she was. Some of them treated me like a celebrity. The chief even asked me for an autograph. As it happened, I had some stills from my movies in my car trunk, which I had put there when I was on my way to a television interview, so I fetched them and signed them for whoever asked.

Donna was beaming the whole time. She had badly wanted to marry Vito, and I hoped he was ready to settle down and not be a philandering husband.His advanced age made me more optimistic than I would have been twenty years earlier. We must've drunk about fifteen or twenty toasts to the happy couple. The mayor's wife, who was quite tipsy, asked Vito why he had waited so long to get married, and he said, "I didn't think I could make it through if I started too *young.*"

"Make it through what?" she asked with an uncomprehending giggle.

"Till death do us part. When they came up with *that* thing in biblical times, people only lived about thirty years. They had an easy row to hoe. We must look at that person for fifty, sixty years or more. Almost nobody can hack it."

"Oh-ho, you joined the married crowd late," the mayor said. "Like those scammers who cheat on running the Marathon by sneaking into it when everyone else is on the last mile."

"Guilty as charged," Vito admitted.

"Oh, honey!" Donna scolded him with a light punch on his arm. The mayor said, "I read in *Reader's Digest* that the purpose of a marriage certificate is to keep people together when they're not in love." We all laughed, recognizing the truth in it.

His wife said, "Remember that other good one, Honey? About kissing?" "I forget. "She said, "Kissing is a way for people to get so close that they can't see anything wrong with each other." This got even more laughs.

Diane and I flashed smiles at each other because we were both content with our marriage.

CHAPTER 24

My life as a freelancer was usually a mad scramble. I always juggled four or five projects at once, somehow keeping all the balls in the air until one of them got sold or financed. It was always hectic, but I preferred it to the alternative of no jobs, no prospects, and no career finished.

In the fall of 1993, I delivered the manuscript of *Day Care* and received the monies owed upon acceptance. On the heels of that, my New York agent landed another three-book deal for me, with an enormous advance and a higher royalty. The good part was that I would have a full year before I was obligated to deliver the first manuscript.

This gave me an interlude for pushing hard on a movie deal, and my Hollywood rep stirred up interest in my script for a unique vampire movie. Its working title was *The Awakening,* but we knew that would have to change because there already had been a Charlton Heston movie of that same title, something about an Egyptian mummy.

My own story was about a doctor named Benjamin Latham, who was hanged in 1776 for doing experiments with human blood. But the mumbo-jumbo performed by the judge, the priest, and the executioner works backward. When Benjamin is buried at a crossroads with a stake in his heart, it causes him to come out of his grave, reborn two centuries later in Pittsburgh. Now, he *does* have a craving for human blood, and when he sees all the evils and excesses of the present day, he decides that plenty of people deserve to be his victims. The novel's overriding theme is the contrast between what America hoped she would become at the time of the Revolution and what she apparently has become thus far in her history. And these philosophical arguments are seen through the eyes of a unique, highly insightful vampire.

As it turned out, after two years of infighting and rewrites at the behest of studio bigwigs, I once again collected several fat chunks of option money. Finally, they said they were in love with the script and that it would soon be green-lighted.

This got my hopes up, but after months more in limbo, the project was dumped when my agent couldn't get any word about its status. And I was almost glad because, in my opinion, the direction the studio forced me to take with the re-writes bastardized the original concept beyond recognition, and the movie I would have had to make for them would have been an abomination. So, I had the money and not the obligation. I consoled myself with one of my favorite sayings: Now and then, a blind pig gets an acorn.

The upshot of all this rigmarole was that I decided that *The Awakening* would make an excellent novel for the first entry into my new three-book deal. I wrote an outline, and my editor loved it. When I submitted the first few chapters, she excitedly phoned me and said, "Aaron, I'm reading the manuscript, and I can't put it down! It's utterly fabulous! Please keep going! I can't wait to read more!"

Half a year later, while I was working on the novel, my Hollywood rep found a small company that wanted to make the movie version, but once again on a meager budget—much lower, in fact, than what was required. But I bit the bullet and took the deal because they would let me work from the original script, not the bastardized rewrites, allowing me to make the picture my way in Pittsburgh.

For the next year and a half, all my time and energy went into that movie. Vito, Joy, and Diane worked hard along with me during pre-production and the entire shooting schedule, and most of the post-production was mainly on my shoulders. I had changed the title from *The Awakening* to *Heartstopper* because the vampire, Benjamin Latham, had come back from the dead with poisonous saliva that stopped people's hearts.

One day, after the editing and mixing had been finalized and the film laboratory was working on color corrections and other technical issues in preparation for turning out the first finished print, I got a phone call from Vito, who was so excited he was almost shouting at me.

"Great news, man! I think we'll be able to reopen the Biff Conley case!"

"What do you mean? You're not back on the police force, are you?"

"C'mon, I'm too old to be a foot soldier. But when I tell them I've got DNA, they'll probably let me work it as a cold case."

"DNA? What are you talking about, Vito? Nobody even knew DNA existed back in 1952."

"But we know about it *now* -- and that's my point. I hate to brag, but I had foresight, man. I ensured all the evidence was locked in a secure case repository back then and kept, not destroyed, since Biff and the other two mooks were convicted. I knew their appeals would wind on and on down through the years, and believe it or not, I had doubts about their guilt, which I couldn't voice openly while I was doing my job, especially on the witness stand. I didn't think the Satanism thing *was* a thing, and new evidence might eventually come to light.

"This is hard to digest suddenly," I told him. "You say we might have DNA after all these years?"

"On a pair of underpants," he said as if pulling a rabbit out of a hat. "Underpants that belonged to one of the boys."

"You *kept* them?"

"Get it in your head, Dave. I made sure the police department kept everything after I left. That includes blood smears from Biff, Howie, and Mo. And guess what? The DNA from the semen stains on the underpants doesn't match the DNA from the blood smears. That could not have been determined back in 1952. But this is 1997. And contrary to what some asshole defense attorneys will argue, DNA doesn't disintegrate, degrade and become useless. It can be tested years, even decades, after the fact. You might remember that during the O.J. Simpson trial, Barry Scheck maintained that the blood spatter in O.J.'s driveway was too degraded to be trusted. But at the same time, he was identifying corpses of soldiers blown apart and buried for months and months on battlefields in Romania. A total hypocrite."

"That's for sure," I said. "But I guess his guilty conscience was bugging him because after he helped get Simpson off, he founded the Innocence Project, and they've started getting convicted murderers out of prison, exonerated by old DNA that's never been tested till now."

"The system is fucked up," Vito said. "It's the worst justice system in existence, as they say, *except* for all the others."

Thinking on a different track, I said, "What if the semen on the underpants was left by someone who wasn't there when the boys were killed?"

"Possible," said Vito. "But who?"

I had no answer.

We both fell silent for a long moment. Then he said, "Let me get back to you. If I can get permission to investigate this as a hired gun, would you want to assist me?

"Does a bear shit in the woods?" I told him.

I had never stopped being appalled and tormented by the murder of my friends.

CHAPTER 25

"We have to distance ourselves," Vito said. "Block out our emotions and treat it like solving a puzzle."

He was temporarily a paid member of the Clairton Police Force again, authorized to work a cold case, and I was his unofficial partner. As a person who had worked homicides for quite a few years, he was used to distancing himself from his emotions, and he was telling me that I had to do the same; in other words, not allow myself to have tunnel vision because we were focusing on the murders of my boyhood friends.

It was a Saturday morning in February 1998, and we were in the lawyers' conference room down the hall from his office. His Murder Book was open in the center of the table, and we both had spiral notebooks, sharpened pencils, and ballpoint pens. At the end of the room, opposite the windows, there was a whiteboard and a trough that held various colored felt markers.

Photos of the three boy victims were taped to the upper part of the board, along with mug shots of Biff, Mo, and Howie.

In the front of the Murder Book was a Case Summary that had been put together as the case was almost ready to go to trial back in 1952. Vito opened the prongs of the binder, took out the summary, and made me a copy on the machine behind him. "Read it over and see if anything stands out," he instructed.

I made notes on the things that I hadn't known before. For instance, I hadn't realized that there had been so many suspects who were ruled out. Two of them, Chris Worthy and Brian

Stanko, both teenagers with a history of drug offenses, had departed on a train to California four days after the bodies were discovered. Worthy was casually familiar with the boys because he used to drive an ice cream truck in their neighborhoods. He and Stanko were arrested and given polygraph exams by police in Santa Clarita, California, and deception was indicated when they were asked about the murders. Worthy claimed he had a long history of drug and alcohol abuse, with blackouts and memory lapses. At one point in his interrogation, he said he "might have" killed the boys, but he quickly recanted.

Another peculiarity of the initial investigation was that an "unknown black male" was reported to have been seen in the ladies' room of a fast-food restaurant. The manager said he appeared to be "mentally disoriented." He was bleeding and had brushed against the restroom walls as he staggered out and was gone. She gave the responding patrolman a pair of sunglasses that she thought were left by the man. The patrol cop took some blood scrapings but later reported that he had lost them. There was nothing to follow up with, and this sketchy lead had been dropped, whether rightly or wrongly.

The part of the Murder Book summary that sharply drew my attention was a paragraph that brought forth the fact that Armand Angelo, Joey Angelo's stepfather, gave a knife to a local news cameraman two days after the bodies were found. The cameraman turned the knife over to a patrolman who was doing crowd control, and Mr. Angelo, who had adopted Joey after marrying his mother, was questioned by Detective Vito Martinelli after a trace of blood was found on the blade. Mr. Angelo claimed that he had cut himself with it. He passed a polygraph test, and the blood sample was too small to be further tested. Detective Martinelli thought there were bite marks on Joey Angelo's face, but when impressions were taken of his stepfather's teeth, a forensic dental expert could not rule

136

either out or in that the impressions matched the marks; they were too faint for a definitive comparison. There was also a belt buckle bruise on Joey's left buttock, and Mr. Angelo admitted that he had "spanked" the boy shortly before he went missing, which might have caused him to hide in the woods.

I said to Vito, "May I ask you something? This guy, Armand Angelo. Did you grill the hell out of him? He was brutal. He beat Joey with the buckle end of a belt, and he admitted it -- called it a spanking, trying to minimize it and make it sound innocent. When I was a kid, my dad told me *his* father beat him with the buckle end of a belt. No wonder my father is so screwed up. He told me he used to run away and sleep in the woods, too scared to go home. Then, when hunger or cold got to him, he'd finally go home and get beaten worse. It sounds like Joey's stepfather was a sonofabitch."

"Yeah," Vito said. "We homed in on Mr. Angelo pretty ferociously till Biff and his buddies became much better suspects."

"What do you think now?" I asked him.

"Maybe we fucked up."

Thinking it over, I said, "This is pure conjecture, but maybe Joey took the opportunity to go down to the shack with the other two boys because he had to get away from his stepfather. And maybe the stepfather came after him and beat up on him some more. Maybe it went too far, and he killed Joey without meaning to. Then he had to get rid of the innocent witnesses."

"Except he passed his polygraph," Vito said. "It's not admissible in court, but it's a useful tool. *Very* useful. It tells us where to look and where not to look. We'd be lost without it. More cases would go unsolved."

However," I said, "there are many cases in which guilty people have passed lie detector tests."

"That's for sure," said Vito. "But we had nothing else to hold Armand Angelo on. And I was getting political pressure to file charges against the others."

I was disappointed in Vito when he virtually admitted he had given in to that kind of pressure, but I didn't say so. I was keenly aware that I had never walked in his shoes. I could only hope that now, at this late date, he and I could resolve the case correctly. It seemed like an uphill climb, but we'd get lucky.

Once more delving into the Murder Book, I learned that yet another knife had figured in the investigation. Pamela Angelo, Joey Angelo's mother, had told Vito that she had found a knife in Armand's nightstand that she knew for sure belonged to Joey. "He always carried it with him. My father gave Joey that knife," Pamela said, "and Joey treasured it as a birthday present from his grandpa. I had assumed the murderer had taken it. I couldn't believe it was among Armand's things. He never told me that he had it."

"Wow!" I said to Vito. "Armand Angelo had Joey's knife that he always carried with him? Didn't that turn up the heat on the   stepfather?"
"Pamela couldn't produce the knife," Vito told me. "We couldn't prove Armand ever had it, and of course, he denied it. Pamela also said that she had seen Armand washing some bloody clothes around the time of the murder, but we couldn't prove that either. We found nothing like that at their house."

"Did she have a motive to lie?"

"Well, Armand was abusing her as well as the boy, according to some of their neighbors. It seemed that she might be making up stories to get him jailed so she could get out of the marriage without having to be scared that he'd come after her. We knew that was exactly what a defense attorney would argue, and it'd likely be enough to get her husband a Not Guilty verdict."

"Where is Mr. Angelo now?" I asked Vito.

"Still married and living with Pamela. He's not in good health. He has diabetes and has had one of his legs amputated."

"I suppose she can stay with him now that she can outrun him," I said. It was a morbid joke, but I had good reason not to sympathize with abusers.

Vito and I discussed everything we knew so far, and he made little charts and notes on the whiteboard.

When we were ready to knock it off and go for a couple of beers at the Terrace Garden, I said, "What about that skull we found that still hasn't been identified?"

"What about it? We're stuck."

"I've heard that DNA can sometimes be extracted from a tooth."

"I already discussed that with a DNA forensic specialist. He said that after all these years, it'd be highly unlikely."

"Maybe he's wrong. Maybe it's worth a shot."

"I doubt it."

I thought this over and said, "Look, I have some extra money, thanks to getting paid on *Heartstopper*. I'll pay for a sketch artist or a computer reconstructive artist to create a likeness. I'd be glad to do that. Maybe it'll help us figure out who the skull belonged to."

"Okay," Vito said. I'll talk to Dr. Kessler at CMU and find out who the best forensic artist is to do it and what we'd have to furnish to get him or her started. Let's go sip a few and talk about it."

We went to the Terrace Garden and sat at the bar. While we waited for our first round, he asked me how Joy was doing.

"Great," I said. "She's about to get her doctorate and looking for her own place. She's got a new boyfriend, who's also been working on a doctorate, and I think they will get engaged."

Vito chuckled, seemingly at nothing, and then he explained. "I see quite a few beautiful, well-groomed young girls walking around with slovenly, dumb-looking guys -- greasy hair, scruffy untrimmed beards, saggy spandex, baggy T-shirts and sneakers that make their feet look as big as barges. I was in a grocery store the other day and walked past three well-dressed girls and they were talking about one of their friends who wasn't there with them. I heard one of them say, Well, Jackie's pretty and smart. She'll have to go out of town to find somebody. All the guys around here are *losers*."

I chuckled wryly, then said, "Well, the girls are getting an education these days, ambitious to make something of themselves. They're the ones going to college. Too many of the young guys are drop-outs or never-starters. They sponge off their girlfriends and treat them like crap; or worse, they physically abuse them."

I ordered another round, and Vito said, "We've got a decision to make about media involvement. It will be futile to try to keep a tight lid on what we're doing. "I'm thinking maybe we should come out with a press conference to let the world know we're re-opening the most famous cold case that's ever happened here. We'd get a ton of bullshit tips, but we also might flush something out. On the other hand, we don't have the manpower to handle a shithouse full of false leads. We'd be swamped before we even got off the ground."

We both fell silent, thinking about the sour ramifications.

I asked, "Do you think we could enlist some off-duty cops to help?"

"Most of the cops in Clairton are already working two jobs to make ends meet. They do their day shift here, for instance, and then they work a night shift over in Glassport or Elizabeth. It's a shame, but that's how it is, David."

"Well, look," I said, "I can ask Diane if she can work a tip line for four or five days, but I don't know if she'll go for it."

"I'll ask Donna, too," said Vito. "She's got vacation time coming to her. She'd rather be fielding calls than selling maternity outfits at Penney's. Especially if it helps us solve a murder case."

CHAPTER 26

I contacted Dr. James Kessler from CMU, and he recommended a forensic artist from the University of Pittsburgh, Dr. Phyllis Markham, to start creating a lifelike facial rendering of the dead person whose skull and bones we had unearthed. They submitted an invoice to me personally for $20,000, and I paid half in advance on the day that I met with them and delivered the artifacts after signing them out of the evidence room in Clairton with Vito's authorization.

We met again three days after our first meeting because by then, they had a chance to do a preliminary evaluation of the task before them.

The two professors were in their mid-forties, which I knew from looking them up online. Kessler looked ten or fifteen years older than his calendar age; in other words, out of shape. I had noted this on the day he and his students came to look for more bones. He was chubby and soft in a red tie, white short-sleeved dress shirt, and gray slacks. Phyllis Markham was well-kept and had a twinkle in her blue eyes that went well with her well-coiffed light-brown hair with blonde highlights. She wore a neat black suit, a white cashmere turtleneck, and a delicate gold necklace.

I was greatly interested in the process they would undertake, and they started their overview by setting the stage for low expectations.

"First of all," Dr. Kessler said, "our task would be much simpler if we knew the person and had a photo of him that we could overlay onto the skull. But in this case, we have a John

Doe, and we're trying to find *out* who he was. And we have no remnants of soft tissue that could have helped us approximate the thickness of flesh on the face. I don't mean to be utterly discouraging, but we *are* starting from scratch."

"However, I have faced these obstacles before," said Dr. Markham, "and there have been times when I've surprised myself with the accuracy of my reconstructions once relatives have come forward to lock down the identification of the actual person. This is the skull of a fine-boned male aged fifteen to thirty. We are sure he was Caucasian. And we estimate his height at five-six to five-ten by the length and thickness of the ulna found at the discovery site."

"Okay," I said (cutting to the chase, as we say in movie production), "I understand the uncertainties, and I'm not asking for miracles, but I do have faith in both of you. You're the best experts I ever would've been able to find. So, how long will it be before your work is done? And how will you handle the obstacles we all agree we're facing?"

"I would say about six weeks because I have classes to teach," Dr. Markham answered faintly. "I've already cleaned the skull and reattached the mandible. I'll insert a pair of prosthetic eyes, then make a plaster cast to work with, not to mar the original skull. I don't want to bore you with further details, though."

"But I like details," I said to her. This is similar to the meetings I always go through with my special makeup effects people. I can be a better director if I know their actions and why.

"Yes, I see that," said Dr. Kessler.

"Well, this *is* the makeup of a sort," conceded Dr. Markham.

"So, what's the essential part of the procedure? "I asked her.

"After the cast is set, I attach colored plastic nubs at twenty-one specific areas based on reference data that has been experimentally worked out over numerous cases and many, many years of forensic work on human remains. These sites represent the average facial tissue thickness for persons of the same sex, race, and age as the person whose remains are in question. This enables me to begin adding features by using modeling clay."

"When you say 'modeling,' that's something I was never good at," I interjected. "My model airplanes used to turn to be ugly monstrosities that wouldn't fly. They'd bump along and go nowhere."

The professors smiled uncertainly while I shut down a flash of childhood memories. Then Dr. Markham continued.

"There's a predetermined protocol for what comes next," she said. "First, the facial muscles are layered down to the neck's soft tissues. Then, the nose and lips are the most difficult because of the possible variations. Still, there are average calculations that will yield the approximate length and width according to the nasal aperture. Then, the muscles related to facial expressions and the soft tissue around the eyes are added. Finally, the entire face is fleshed, meaning that clay is added until the tissue thickness markers are covered, and also specific characterization is added, like hair, wrinkles in the skin, racial traits, and so on."

"It seems to me that a great deal of intuition must be involved," I remarked. "Coupled with impressive skill, of course."

Dr. Kessler said, "You've hit the nail on the head, David. It might interest you that the famous bust of Mozart we've seen was not made while he was alive. It was a facial reconstruction from anthropological data and did not exist during his lifetime. It was unveiled in Paris in 1991."

"Wow! Thanks. I like knowing things like that," I told him.

We chatted a bit more, getting to know each other a bit more over coffee and croissants brought in by a student, and then I headed home, more anxious than ever to see the skull brought to life, so to speak.

CHAPTER 27

Vito and I met once again in the conference room at his office to form a schedule for interviewing the list of people who had made it into our notes and onto the whiteboard. We realized that we would have to do it together instead of splitting up to make the task go faster because I needed an official status in the investigation. In other words, nobody pinned a deputy badge on me like they might've done in the Old West.

Once more, we decided to postpone setting up a press conference because, so far, we had only identified four people who needed to be re-interviewed. We hoped we'd get by with doing that much without stirring up a beehive. Then, if the media started to notice what we were doing, it would force us out in the open. But at least we would have some degree of confidentiality at the outset.

Our first persons of interest were Chris Worthy and Brian Stanko, the two druggies who had skipped to California four days after the kids' bodies were discovered. Worthy, I readily recalled, was the one who used to drive an ice cream truck. Vito pulled up their rap sheets and vital statistics, read his computer screen for a while, shook his head, and said, "They're both long gone. I overdosed on heroin way back in the eighties. I hope they weren't the real killers because if so, everybody else we look at is gonna be a waste of time."

"Were they living in California when they O.D.'d?" I asked Vito. "Or did they come back here at some point?"

"No, they both died in Muscle Beach. They hustled the gay bodybuilders, and they both got AIDS. Back when it was a sure death sentence. A heroin overdose might've seemed like a preferable way out."

"Yikes," was my muted comment.

"Anyhow," Vito said, "before we go gallivanting all over the United States, we ought to cover the leads that are nearby -- like right here in Clairton or not far from here. Let's list those possibilities and see which ones we can easily get in touch with."

Consulting the whiteboard and the case summary in the Murder Book, these were the targets we came up with:

(1)   ARMAND ANGELO. Joey Angelo's stepfather. He is known to have given the boy a beating with the buckle end of a belt on the day he first went missing.

(2)   PAMELA ANGELO. Joey's mother. She and her sister had claimed to have found Joey's knife, the one he got from his grandfather, in Armand Angelo's nightstand. They also had told a story, whether real or made up, that they had seen Armand washing some bloody clothes.

(3)   MARY ANN SUMPTER. She had furnished incriminating testimony in Biff and the boy's first trial that helped put them away. Many years later, she had recanted, which had helped get them freed.

(4) THERESA CORRADO. The owner of the little store by the peach orchard told the police that she had seen and heard Armand Angelo in the alley calling Joey's name on the day he went missing.

Those four were the ones we initially needed to talk to, and whatever they had to say at this late date might give us a wedge to jog their memories and provoke more leads. At least it was a starting point. But seeing only four names on our agenda at the outset made me wonder if we had much hope of accomplishing anything. But Vito didn't seem discouraged,

147

perhaps because he was used to homicide cases that looked hopeless till he started digging.

He said, "Let's hold off on the stepfather till we talk to the others first. Maybe we'll get some info that will help us pressure him. He looks like he might be carrying the most guilt, even if he didn't kill the three boys. He's had to live with the knowledge that he beat the hell out of Joey on the last day the boy was on this earth."

"So, if not him, who do we start with?" I asked him.

"Let's start with the ones that seem easy," he said. "I mean, the ones probably have no reason to fear us. Theresa Corrado and Mary Ann Sumpter, whose last name was Seidling when she came in and recanted."

"You don't think Mary Ann will be spooked?"

"Maybe a little, but we'll tell her we just want to clear up a few things and see if we can ask her some questions that might jog her memory a bit more."

I opened my laptop so I could help Vito with the Googling chores. Without much trouble, I ascertained that Mary Ann Sumpter was now 64 years old, was still living in Clairton, and was still married to Charles Seidling, a foreman at the Irvin Works of U.S. Steel, but had recently retired. My dad always bitched about the foremen he worked under, and I didn't recall him ever bitching about Charles or Chuck Seidling, so he might not have ever known him, which was lucky for Chuck.

The Seidlings didn't owe any back taxes or have no liens against them. They lived on a decent side street, Baker Avenue, about two blocks from American Legion Post 75, to which Vito and I belonged. Their home phone number was listed. Vito tried it after putting me on speakerphone, and a man answered. He said, "I'm their son, Matthew. My mom's home, but my dad's out. Hold on, I'll get her. Who should I say is calling?"

"Vito Martinelli. She knows me."

Within a few minutes, Mary Ann got on the line. She didn't sound frazzled, so I thought maybe having a clean conscience had calmed her down. Vito told her what he wanted, and she asked if he wanted her to come to his office or to her place and when.

He said, "Is maybe now a good time?"

After a pause, she said, "I guess so."

Baker Avenue was only five minutes away by car, up the hill past the American Legion and the football stadium. The Seidlings' home was a two-story colonial with white siding and green trim, including green faux shutters. It was on the left side of the street, which was the side where all the houses had terraces and single-car garages with uphill driveways; on the other side, the properties were level, as on Farnsworth Avenue, where I grew up.

By now, it was March 1998, and it was quite windy. They came in like a lion, as usual. If Vito and I had been wearing hats, they would have blown off our heads. As it was, our hair was blown wild. He pressed a button, and we heard a bell from inside. Mary Ann came to the door, led us inside, and offered coffee and cake. We accepted the snack without demur to get the interview started in an amicable way.

She said, "I'll bring it out. We can sit at the dining table."

Although she had major issues in her childhood, which led her to be easily manipulated by Biff Conley if I had not known that part of her history, I would have seen her as simply an ordinary, self-assured elderly adult comfortable with having us in her home.

As she emerged from the kitchen with a tray holding the coffee service and slices of yellow cake with white icing, she said, "Sorry, I'm not more presentable. Today is my day for dusting and sweeping." She wore a pink sweatshirt and jeans, and her brown hair was pinned back and probably chemically darkened.

149

"You look fine," Vito assured her.

She said, "My son Matthew answered the phone when you called. Then he went up to the American Legion. My husband goes up there to play cards. If we're going to talk about anything from my unfortunate past, let's do it while they're not here."

We ate cake and sipped coffee as we talked. The room was attractively appointed, and the furniture wasn't cheap. The pale blue curtains were pulled aside, allowing a cheerful sunlight ambiance.

Vito said, "Mary Ann, rest assured, we're not here to make you uncomfortable. The past is the past and what's done is done. We know you're a good person. I don't think we have to rehash your statements at the first trial, when you had to say what you did because of threats

from Spencer Conley."

"Biff. That's how I knew him," she said. "I never knew his real first name till it was in the newspaper. And at first, I didn't realize that's who they were talking about."

"Understandable," said Vito. "You were only fourteen years old. You were a victim."

I let him ask all the questions while I took notes on a little spiral notebook, like the ones I had seen detectives use in the movies—even in my own movies. I could have used my laptop, but I felt more like doing it the old-fashioned way, which also seemed less intrusive.

"I had no self-confidence back then," Mary Ann said.

"You lived in fear and self-doubt," Vito acknowledged. "And when a person is in that constantly disruptive state of mind, a fight-or-flight mechanism kicks in. It blocks a lot of things out. I'm wondering if perhaps if you make an effort, you may recall something that was on the fringes of your mind back then but failed to penetrate because you were too pent-up to register it consciously."

"I think I follow you," she said. "But it sounds like you're talking about something that might require hypnosis. Something I've always been afraid of, and I don't exactly know why."

I could see that she was quite intelligent and articulate, and those factors helped her pull herself up by her bootstraps.

Vito said, "Hypnosis has occurred to me, but I don't think it'd be productive without having an idea of what we'd be trying to get at. So, let me try to be more specific. When you came forward and recanted, did you mean to naysay *all* of your original testimony, or were parts of it truer than others?"

"Like what?" she said, biting her lip and appearing utterly puzzled.

"Well, maybe Biff didn't say or do some of the more bizarre things you accused him of, but maybe the other two did. In other words, it should have helped free Biff when you recanted, but not necessarily all three of them.

"I see what you're saying," Mary Ann said thoughtfully. "But none of them bragged about killing anybody. I was so screwed up back then I made it up. I was ashamed of what they knew about me, having sex with all of them whenever they wanted it, and I wanted them out of my life. Putting them in prison was my way of achieving that. I still never get a good night's sleep because I feel so guilty for what I did to them."

Vito said, "We're all pretty dumb when we're kids, Mary Ann. And you were a kid from a bad family situation, and you were highly vulnerable. It would be best if you forgave yourself at long last. You took the first step when you recanted. I don't mean to dredge it all up for you all over again. I want to be sure that none of the three should still be in prison."

"But if I had come forward sooner, Mo would still be alive," Mary Ann said, and she started to cry. She let the tears fall and didn't bother to wipe them. Her voice became more

151

strident and self-accusatory. "It's *my* fault! They were *bad* kids, but no worse than *me!* They didn't deserve the punishment I *caused!* None of them killed anybody! *None* of them!"

Sobs wracked her, and Vito got up and put a hand on her shoulder. Then he bent and hugged her and let her cry. In a while, she stopped sobbing and pulled herself together bit by bit.

I wished I could do something, but I didn't know what. I stopped taking notes. There needed to be something pertinent enough to write down.

CHAPTER 28

After Mary Ann Seidling, the next person Vito and I wanted to talk to was Theresa Corrado, the owner of the little store in the alley behind Farnsworth Avenue. Every family on the street frequented her store when I was growing up. It was at the head of a row of garages that people could rent for five bucks a month to have a place to park their cars because parking on the front street wasn't allowed for those families who lived on the side of Farnsworth opposite the Cristi house. The ones who didn't want to pay the five dollars sometimes parked in their backyards, which were so small that the car took up the whole lawn. The garage building was partitioned by only chicken wire to separate the rental units, was of wood planks painted gray, with a tarpaper roof, often with strips of the tarpaper blown off.

Theresa was a kindly, cheerfully enterprising lady who owned the garages and the store. She allowed the housewives on the street to run a tab, which she required to be paid in full every two weeks because the men working in the mills got paid in cash twice a month. As a little boy, when my mom walked up to the store, leaving me home alone, I would excitedly watch through the front window for her return, anxious to see what she had bought and if it was anything I liked. I loved banana flip cakes in a cellophane package, a pasty yellow cake with chemically created icing rolled inside that I wouldn't go near today. On paydays, I could barely wait to dig into the little paper bag of candy that Theresa gave her and every other mom each time they paid their tab.

Nostalgia gripped me as Vito and I walked up the alley and past the garages, the big gray doors locked and hasped. Some of my boyhood friends' names were carved with penknives into the wood and could still be made out, even though they had been painted over numerous times, mostly their nicknames: RONYAY, DING, TEELA, FICO, and many more. Quite a few were dead, and some had died very young. Some had drowned in the river.

We had been especially cruel to Teela, whose real name was Dickie Slovko. When we were in grade school, some kids mocked him by calling him "Teela" after the elephant in the Tarzan movies. He wasn't even grossly fat, just chubby. But a congenital heart problem ran in his family, and he couldn't run fast without losing his breath. We used to race en masse up to the Five Corners of the street to see who would be "it" in whatever game we were about to play. But eventually, we stopped racing because it was such a foregone conclusion that either Dickie or a much fatter kid nicknamed, naturally, Porky would always be last. So, from then on, only the two of them raced while the rest of us walked and still got there ahead of them. More childhood cruelty that didn't faze us at the time. But his father died young, and so did he. He didn't make it past age fifty.

Seeing all those familiar childhood names carved into the gray wood made me think of one of my favorite poems by Alfred Edward Housman, which I knew by heart, from his book of verse called *A Shropshire Lad*:

With rue my heart is laden
For golden friends I had,
For many a rose-lipped maiden
And many a lightfoot lad.

By brooks too broad for leaping
The lightfoot lads are laid

The rose-lipped maids are sleeping
In fields where roses fade.

I didn't know if anybody still rented the chicken-wire garages, but Theresa Corrado was still running the store even though she was way up in years. She was expecting us. Everything in there was old and cramped; after Vito and I were inside, there was practically no room for anyone else, but there were no other customers. There was little on the shelves. Theresa was gray, withered, and bent over.

The cooler in the narrow aisle in front of the wooden counter looked like the same one that was there when I was a kid. It had a smeary glass top, and I could see a few popsicles in there, so I bought a sticky cherry one and had difficulty peeling off the wrapper. I bit into it while Theresa fawned over me and rehashed fond memories of what kind of boy I had been and how wonderful it was that I was now making movies. She also fawned a little over Vito because she knew who he was, that he had been a cop, and she and his mother had been church ladies together.

She stayed behind the small counter, and Vito and I remained standing because there was nowhere to sit. After the chit-chat, Vito asked her, "Do you remember much about the day Ron, Mickey, and Joey went missing?"

"I'll never forget it," she said, crossing herself, almost ready to cry.

"Can you tell us as much as you remember?" Vito asked.

"I told it all at the trial. It had nothing to do with the three killers."

"You still think they're guilty?"

"Well, aren't they? I can tell you for sure none of them were any damn good!"

"What makes you say that, Theresa?"

155

"They were always stealing from me. Shoplifting. Many times, I had to chase them out of there, and they'd run down the alley. The cops wouldn't do anything because they missed them in the act."

"But it's a far cry from a bit of shoplifting to multiple murders," Vito said.

"Those bullies were always picking on younger kids, too," Theresa said adamantly. "It was only a matter of time before they hurt one of them really bad."

"Well, let's talk about your trial testimony," Vito suggested.

"I didn't see them do anything, mind you. I could tell that the defense lawyer wanted me to say things about Armand Angelo. But I didn't see him do much either."

"I know you've told it before," Vito said. "I just want to hear some details that weren't covered back then."

A bit miffed, she said, "Well, I don't know what *that* would be! Both those lawyers grilled me as if I was John Dillinger!"

I had my pen and notepad out, but so far, I had yet to write down anything.

Vito said, "Who did you see in the alley that day?"

"Lots of people. I had customers then, different from now. They all drive to the mall. That day, quite a few mothers came to the store or sent their kids to pick up a couple of odds and ends they maybe forgot they needed for Easter."

"But only one person was looking for one of the missing boys, right?"

"You mean Armand Angelo."

"Yes. According to your testimony, he was calling for Joey, his stepson. You heard him from the alley, right?"

Now, we were getting to the crux of the matter, so I began taking notes.

"*Saw* him, too," Theresa said. "He was bellowing like an ox. So loud, I came out to see what was going on. He had a belt with a big buckle in his right hand, swinging it as he

156

walked. And he was stomping, not just walking, and yelling Joey's name repeatedly."

"He sounded angry?"

"Darn right, he did. The defense attorney made me say that a couple of times till the other attorney objected. I knew what the defense attorney was up to; he was trying to make people think Armand might've been mad enough to kill. But he was only Joey's stepfather; he had nothing to do with the other two boys. So why would he have killed them? That's what was brought out in closing arguments. The Satanism thing and the drinking of human blood, which Mary Ann Sumpter told, convinced those jurors as to who made the killings -- and the mutilations. Why would a simple mill worker like Mr. Angelo do that?"

"Mary Ann has admitted that she lied back then," Vito told her.

"Hmph! I believe she told the *truth* back then and is lying *now!* Her mother used to shoplift here and tried it too, but I caught her. I never trusted any*body* in that family!"

"Okay," Vito said. "I appreciate your taking the time to talk with us."

He handed her his card and told her to phone him if she thought of anything, and we left. Remembering how we used to have access to the little peach orchard and the path behind the store, I thought of something that all of us boys used to laugh about way back then when it wasn't anything to laugh about. It was the day Buddy O'Riley, nicknamed B.O., was carried out of the woods face down on a stretcher as the result of a blasting cap accident in one of our war games. Ronyay, whose real name was Ronald Danko, was on the side that hid, and B.O. was on the side trying to find them. We used the blasting caps to simulate land mines. The idea was to bury a blasting cap and then detonate it when the "enemy troop" had passed over it but had gotten a safe distance of ten or fifteen feet away. But Ronyay forgot precisely where he had buried the cap and set it off when B.O was right over it. It went off, sending him sprawling with his toy rifle and blasting his butt with shrapnel. But this sounds worse than it was. The "shrapnel" was mostly dirt and small stones, and he recovered in a few days.

I used to love those war games when I was a kid because the Korean War was on, and I wished I was old enough to have the "adventure" of fighting the Red Chinese. Back then, I really had no idea how awful war was. One of my favorite writers, Ernest Hemingway, was just that naive when he was only eighteen and volunteered to fight with the Italians in World War One. But at least he had the adventure, and it was part of the mythology he built around himself, the mystique that he was not only an acclaimed author but a worldly adventurer.

Vito and I walked down the alley to the small field where I used to play sandlot football with my friends, none of us wearing helmets or shoulder pads. That's where I had parked my car. I doubted that any of the kids nowadays have ever played tackle football or anything else, and the sparse grass didn't look trampled. When I say sparse, I mean there were bare spots, nothing there but clay and stones and even pieces of glass. I got tackled and fell on a chunk of glass one day and still had a scar on the palm of my right hand.

I wondered if any kids nowadays ever built shacks or stole bull ropes to make swings in the woods. But on the other hand, probably none of them ever got blown up by a blasting cap or drowned in the river.

Maybe they didn't even know how to swim. It's hard to learn things like that when all your time is spent playing video games.

CHAPTER 29

Based on what Theresa Corrado had said, plus what was in the Murder Book about Armand Angelo, we were anxious to talk with him. But Vito thought it might be best if we spoke with his wife first. If he had abused both her and Joey, she might be ready to open up at long last.

We discovered that Armand's wife, Pamela, was working at one of the gambling joints on St. Clair Avenue, a block from downtown Miller Avenue, the main street of town. There were fifteen or twenty such places all over Clairton, an open secret, raided every now and then by the State Police but otherwise left alone, so long as cash was paid under the table to the politicians and the police. They usually called themselves "coffee shops," and they did serve coffee and doughnuts and often sold potato chips and newspapers, but little else. Their main source of illegal cash was poker machines, and each coffee shop had a bank of them, usually anywhere from six to twelve machines that occasionally paid out big jackpots. Still, usually not, because they weren't there to pay out, they were there to take people's money. Each joint also harbored a "street person" who loafed there all day long, seven days a week, and took numbers bets and sports bets. A dollar hit on the State lottery paid $500, but a dollar hit on the illegal, untaxed numbers paid $600 and sometimes $700.

Vito wanted me to case the L&M Coffee Shop, where Pamela Angelo worked, so I went in alone one day, ostensibly to say hello to old pals. There were always a few of them in there, drinking coffee, smoking cigarettes, bullshitting, and working crossword puzzles.

Pamela was behind the coffee counter. The joint's bookie, Matt McCoy, son of Ray McCoy, now deceased, who used to be called Horseshit McCoy and absolutely hated it, was sitting at a table by himself, doing nothing. Four of my old pals were playing penny-ante poker at another table, and they perked up big-time as soon as they saw me. One of them said, "Well, hello, Hollywood, what brings *you* here? Slumming?" His comment had an edge of nastiness, but I pretended not to notice.

I detoured to the counter because, at the moment, no one was sitting there. Pamela Angelo came over to me. She didn't look much like her photo in the Murder Book, having aged almost fifty years, which put her in her mid-seventies. Her face was a mass of wrinkles, a smoker's face, and she was puffing away right now with an ashtray full of butts in front of her. Her gray hair was in a short frizz. She wore a blue sweater and brown slacks. I ordered black coffee and a doughnut, and when she brought it to me, I took my opportunity to speak to her in a low voice. "Vito Martinelli would like to talk with you in private. Do you know where his office is?"

She darted her eyes around and spoke in a near whisper. "What's this all about?"

"A few questions about your son's case. We're trying to open up some new leads."

"You're wasting your time," she said angrily. Nothing new is going to happen, and nothing good is going to happen anyway."

"I'm sorry for your loss," I told her. I know it still hurts. But the reason we're opening the case again is that we already have some new evidence."

She thought about it, looking nervous. Then she said, "Is it okay if I come to Vito's office tomorrow? It's my day off."

I said, "That'd be great. What time is good for you?"

"How about ten o'clock? Does my husband have to know about this?"

"Not if you don't want him to."

"I don't."

"He won't hear about it from us. That I can guarantee."

I took my coffee and doughnut over to where the card game was happening, sat on a chair nearby, and chatted for a while with the players. Out of an ingrained habit, I was careful not to appear as if I was looking over any of their shoulders at their cards; in my youth, any suspicion of that sort of thing was almost guaranteed to get a person clobbered.

I easily recalled the names of two of the players but not the other two, though I knew them all and should have remembered their names but couldn't. They still knew me on sight as well as they used to because of my movies. If I hung around much longer without using their names, they would figure me for somebody who had turned snobbish.

I got out of there, anxious to hear what Pamela would tell us the next morning.

***

She was late getting to Vito's office, and we were figuring her as a no-show and trying to decide what to do about it when she finally arrived with a cigarette sticking out of her lips. She was wearing the same blue sweater and brown slacks she had on yesterday. Vito ushered her into the conference room where I was already seated, and the first thing she said was, "Do I have to put this out?"

Vito said, "No, let me find you an ashtray." He left the room to hunt for one.

161

I knew that the entire law office building was a no-smoking zone, but Vito wanted her to feel as unwary as possible, so he didn't want to tell her so. "Good morning," I told her. Thanks for coming in. Please be comfortable. Take a seat, Pam." She did so rather awkwardly and plunked down a ratty-looking purse made of scarred black vinyl.

There were no ashtrays in the building, which was no surprise. When Vito came back, he had a glass candy dish in his hand, which he set down in front of Pamela. She immediately used it to stub out a butt, then rummaged in her purse for a Bic and a pack of unfiltered Camels and lit up another one. The air in the conference room soon started to smell harsh, and as an ex-smoker of twenty years, I wondered why I had ever done it, especially when Pamela began coughing.

"Should I get you some water?" Vito asked.

She shook her head no, her face red, and still coughing. But she got it under control and took another deep drag, held it in with some difficulty, then exhaled another toxic cloud.

Vito said, "I'd like to begin by asking you what you remember when your son went missing. I'm sorry if it's painful, but it's part of our search for justice."

She didn't blink at that. I got ready to take notes.

She said, "How far back do you want to go?"

Vito said, "If anything sticks in your mind that happened in the lead-up to that day, please tell me about it. Even if it seems outwardly unimportant." She sucked in another drag and stared away from Vito contemplatively. Then she said, "Armand gave Joey a beating. But he wouldn't tell me why. He said I didn't need to know."

"Where did this happen?"

"In Joey's bedroom. I could hear him yelling, and I didn't know what to do. I knew if I went up there, he'd turn on *me*. Then he'd beat Joey worse. That's what always happened."

"Does he still beat you?"

"No. Because he needs me too much. Now that he has a missing leg. He also has a colostomy bag. I have to do things for him that nobody else would do."

"Okay," said Vito. "I understand. He's lucky to have you, Pamela. But why did you stay with him, even when he was beating you and your son?"

This line of questioning naturally hit me in a soft spot, and I did my best to ignore my personal feelings and write things down as dispassionately as possible.

Pamela's answer was pretty close to what my mother might have said.

"Where could I go, and what could I do? My first husband was a good man, but he died at a young age, only twenty-seven, from a brain aneurism, a total shock. Armand was all sugar and cream when he started dating me. He didn't turn on me and Joey till after we were married by a justice of the peace. Not long after, either. At least if I stuck with him, Joey and I would have a roof over our heads. Armand owned the house. Before that, we were in a high-rise in Blair, down with the niggers."

I blanched at that. So did Vito. I saw him blink and try to cover up a grimace. But we couldn't get tough with her now because we still needed her. There wasn't as much racial prejudice in Clairton as there used to be, but there was still plenty, especially among older people. My father was a prime example. He hated Martin Luther King and Jesse Jackson. His racist diatribes could ruin a family dinner. One time, I told him I was going to bring him a white pointy hood with eye slits. I always tried to get him not to use the "N" word around Joy when she was little, but I seldom succeeded.

"Were you sorry you married Armand Angelo?" Vito asked Pamela.

"I was, and I wasn't. At least he was a good provider."

So was my father, I thought to myself—a good provider of food, clothing and bruises.

"How often did he beat you, Pam?"

She didn't answer right away, perhaps deciding to soften her answer. "Uh...I guess maybe every two or three months or so. In between times, he was nice as pie, but I didn't know how to make those times last. So, I had to take the good with the bad. I felt worse when he took his anger out on my son. Joey was a gentle boy, not a roughneck like most around here. He didn't deserve that kind of stepfather."

"All right, just to clarify," Vito said, "Armand gave Joey a beating the day he went missing, but he wouldn't tell you why. Is that correct?"

"Uh-huh."

"Did he *ever* tell you? If not that day, maybe later? Maybe even years later?"

"No, he refuses to talk about it. He says it hurts him too badly, and he wishes he had done differently because then Joey might still be alive. He says it's his fault my son ran off that day, and somebody did those bad things to him."

Vito allowed a long moment to go by without any questions. Then he said, "Now, this is the hard part, Pam, but I'm afraid it's necessary. Back then, you initially told me that you found Joey's penknife in with some of Armand's possessions. And you also indicated that you had seen him washing some bloody clothes furtively. But later on, you said that neither of those things were true. Do you still stand by that? Or would you rather go back to your original statement? Don't worry, we'll not charge you with perjury; we're just after the truth."

Pam had filled the candy dish with crumpled butts and black residue by now, but she shook yet another Camel from her wrinkled pack and got it burning as fast as she could, and sucked in a lung-full. She slowly let it out without coughing,

164

surprised me, and said, "Betty and I both lied. I talked her into it. I wanted to get Armand jailed, at least for a little while so that I could divorce him. I hated his guts right then because he beat Joey and made him run off."

"Do you still hate Armand? Do you harbor any suspicions about him?"

"What do you mean?"

"Do you believe there's a chance that he killed your son?"

"I used to wonder, I admit, but I don't anymore. He's been a bully and would probably still be one if he wasn't a shell of himself these days. But he's a coward. I don't think he'd have the guts to kill anybody. Certainly not three boys."

Vito sat back and would probably have taken a deep breath if the room wasn't so smoke-filled. He eyed Pamela in a kindly way and said, "All right, Pam, thanks again for coming in. We have some other people we're going to talk to, and then we might want to talk with you again. Is that okay with you?"

"Yeah, I guess," she said. Not enthusiastic.

"Thanks, we appreciate that," Vito told her in all sincerity. "A lot of years have passed, and we can't do anything about that. But we think justice is still possible."

"I hope so," she said. "But I have my doubts."

Vito asked her what sort of condition we could expect to find her husband in if we just showed up at the house without any advance warning, and he asked her not to tell him we were coming. She answered his questions and seemed totally willing to cooperate. She fumbled for another cigarette and lit it up before she went out the door.

Vito hurried up and emptied the candy dish into a wastebasket, stared at it to ensure nothing was still burning, then pulled the entire liner out and closed it tight by twisting it into a knot.

"He said, "Let's get the fuck outta here, Dave, and go someplace where we can breathe. This conference room might be polluted from now till doomsday. If we have to question her again, I'll ensure we meet her in the open air, maybe in Clairton Park."

CHAPTER 30

The day after Pamela's interview, we ensured she was working behind the counter at the coffee shop at nine a.m., and then we barged in on her husband. Or at least that's how it must have felt to him, and we wanted it that way. We wanted him badly shaken and vulnerable.

We didn't break the door down, as in a no-knock narcotics raid. Vito rang the bell, and we waited. We had asked Pamela not to tell him we were coming, and we had a degree of faith that she had complied. It took Armand five or six minutes to answer the bell, which we assumed was because of his prosthetic. His wife had told us he would have it on; she would help him with it before she left for work at the coffee shop.

He knew who we were, and his eyes widened, recognizing us as he swung the door open. Of course, he would've seen both of us on TV in connection with various news reports. But Vito introduced us by name anyway. "Good morning, Mr. Angelo. I'm Vito Martinelli, and this is David Cristi, who is assisting me informally. Your son's case is being reopened due to the emergence of certain previously unknown evidence. May we come in?"

With obvious reluctance, he nodded affirmatively and held the door open. Because of his artificial leg and its attachments, he walked with a rolling gait, like a sailor. He led us into the living room and didn't offer anything. He sat on his recliner with the footstool up, and Vito and I sat on the couch.

His first words were, "You spoke to my wife?" His voice was weak and scratchy.

"No, not yet," Vito lied, taking a chance that she hadn't told him the opposite. But if he believed we *would* speak with her, perhaps he wouldn't outright lie to us.

"What's this new evidence?" he asked gruffly.

For a man with an amputated leg and a colostomy bag, he certainly didn't seem as submissive as I might have expected. I had been aware of the odor of urine as he led us in and maybe a bit of a smell of feces. His brown trousers were rumpled and soiled, and he was wearing a flannel shirt and a black sweater with white stains on it, maybe egg whites. It was warm in the room, with the sun coming through an open curtain, but he must have been cold despite that. He was eighty years old now, mostly bald, and the fringes of gray hair that were poorly left needed a trim. He needed a shave as well. His hazel eyes were dull and watery, and his jowls sagged. His face didn't have any firmness left in it.

Vito said, "I'm not at liberty to reveal what we know at this point, but we've presented it to the proper authorities, and it was enough to reopen the case."

"What're you, a cold-case guy now? You were a cop, then a private eye, is what I heard."

"I'm still a private investigator, but that doesn't stop me from taking on these challenges."

Mr. Angelo thought this over briefly, then said, "Well, fire away, but I'm not gonna say anything different from what I had to say forty-some years ago. I told the truth then, and I'll tell the truth now."

"That's certainly all we expect you do," Vito said. "We can't ask for anything more. We want to review the facts as you know them, hoping you might think of something that didn't seem important to you back then."

"What was important to me was that my stepson was dead!" he suddenly said, not loudly, but with sudden anger. "And those three young bastards slashed him and killed him! I thought they got what they deserved and were put away for good, then they got let out and put back on the streets as if they were poor little lambs! Well, they're *not*. One of them couldn't stomach goin' around in front of us with his guilty conscience, so he hanged himself. If the other two had any decency, they'd follow suit."

I had just taken notes, but I jotted down the gist of that diatribe. Rather than argue with it, Vito played his hole card to knock Armand off his game in case he had any reason to be fearful. "Some of our new evidence that got the case reopened," Vito said, "is DNA evidence. It was found on Joey's underpants."

This dropped bomb didn't make Armand flinch. It seemed that he must know that the DNA couldn't be his. But I needed clarification on that. Maybe he was as unshakable as a deadpan poker player.

"Contrary to popular belief, DNA doesn't deteriorate," Vito persisted. "Not if it's taken good care of. And this specimen was. I made sure of that."

"Good for you," Armand said perfunctorily. "But I've got nothing to worry about. If you were as smart as you think you are, you'd be getting DNA samples from the three killers. You could even exhume the dead one who bumped himself off and get his. I've seen that done on television."

"Television and real life are two different things," Vito said. "But you're right, DNA can be extracted from a corpse, but formaldehyde makes it close to useless in most cases. But we don't need to attempt that. We already have blood smears on slides that were made way back when they were already tested, and none of them match what's on the underpants. That's why we know we're looking for an unknown killer. Somebody who got away with it up till now."

He said this with a hard stare focused on Armand Angelo's slack, withered face. But once again, Armand didn't seem fazed.

"Let me ask you something else," Vito said. "At the time your stepson 's body was found along with the other two victims before anyone was arrested, your wife and her sister both told me that you had Joey's knife and also that they had caught you washing clothing that had blood on it --"

"Those two bitches *lied!*" Armand interrupted angrily. "You never found any knife and no bloody clothing -- and you damn well *know* it! That's because there wasn't any! I should have told you to shove your goddamn search warrant up your ass!"

"Well, in effect, you did," Vito said mildly. "But I assured you that I was just doing my job. And the fact that I *didn't* find what the two women said I *would* find is partly why you got eliminated as a suspect."

"I got eliminated because I was telling the fucking *truth!*" Armand shouted.

"Well, look," Vito said, still trying to be a calming influence in the interest of getting straight answers, "I hereby apologize for any mistakes I made back then. But, since the DNA doesn't match any of the three young men who were convicted, it means that the real killer is still out there if he hasn't passed away. He's gotten away with a triple murder all this time. That's not justice, and I'm a seeker of justice. I want the truth to come out, and I think you and your wife want the same thing."

"That's for damn sure," Armand agreed. "What else do you need to ask me? I hate to say it, but I'm gonna need to empty my fucking bag."

Vito acted as if he didn't get it. He faked a quizzical expression with raised eyebrows.

"I have to wear a fucking colostomy bag," Armand said. "Sometimes I'd rather be dead."

"I'm sorry to hear that," said Vito, sounding sincere. "Can we sneak in just two more questions? If they lead somewhere, we can either wait while you do what you must, or we can leave and return later."

"Go ahead; I think I can manage," Armand said with obvious discomfort.

"Okay, I'll hurry it up. When you went out hunting for Joey and calling for him, did you have any idea where he might have gone, or were you flying blind?"

"No, the first place I'd always look is down by that shack. I hated for him to go down there because it was a good place to get attacked by a pervert. I went to the top of the hill, behind the store and the peach orchard, and kept calling. But nobody yelled back. So, I didn't bother going down there."

"If, as you feared, Joey had been unlucky enough to meet up with a pervert, why wouldn't you have gone down there on the chance that he was in that kind of trouble, and you could've saved him?"

Armand shook his head dolefully and wiped his eyes as if he was about to shed tears.

He said, in a weak, sad voice, "You don't know how many times I've tortured myself, wishing I would've done that. But hindsight is twenty-twenty. I go to confession, and my priest tells me I need to stop beating myself up."

"Last question for now," Vito said. "Assuming that the wrong fellows were put in prison for a long time and didn't deserve it, is there anybody else you think we should be looking at?"

It didn't take Armand long to come up with a name. "That fucking English teacher," he said. "That fucking pansy, Brevko, the English teacher, so smooth his sick mouth wouldn't melt butter. That's who I thought could've done it right from

171

the beginning. He's a pervert. Taking naked pictures of little kids maybe doing worse to them. But he ran away before being *put* away, and nobody seems to know where he's at."

"Let me ask you something that might save us coming back later," Vito said. "Would you mind letting me take a swab for DNA purposes?"

"Not a problem."

Vito already had the swab in a plastic bag in his inner suit-coat pocket. He took it out of the bag, told Armand to open his mouth, and ran the swab around the inside of his mouth. Then he put the swab in the tube and the whole works inside the plastic evidence bag.

"Thanks for being so cooperative," he told Armand. "I greatly appreciate it."

Armand looked at me and said, "You can return the favor. I have a friend who's one of your biggest fans. He watches your movies over and over, all by himself. He has VHS's, DVD's and those new things called some Ray."

I said, "BluRays."

"Yeah, that's it. They keep comin' out with new stuff to make people spend more money. Anyhow, David, my young friend, would go bonkers if I could get him an autograph from you."

I said, "How about a signed photo? I have some in my car trunk."

"That's great, man, I'll pay you for it."

"No need to."

I went out to the car, got one of my stills and a Sharpie in the box, and went back into the house. It was a photo of the actor who played Wayne Calley in full costume, ear necklace and all, making as if to slit my throat with his bayonet. "Should I personalize it or just sign it?" I asked Armand.

"Just your signature is perfect," he said. "My friend is gonna love this."

At this point in my career, I had signed thousands of photos, but this was the first time I had handed one to a murder suspect.

We returned to Vito's office, where he called the lab technician to do the DNA analysis on Armand Angelo's swab. Vito pushed hard, but the technician said there was so much of a backload he couldn't guarantee anything for six or seven weeks.

When Vito got off the line, he smiled and said, "Six or seven weeks is better than I hoped for. I will expedite this for overnight delivery, so nothing holds it up."

"What did you think of Armand Angelo?" I asked him.

"He's believable, but he's lying."

"That was my take, too. But *why* is he lying? How guilty do you think he is? And of what? Beating Joey with a belt buckle and making him run away, or something worse?"

"I don't know yet. We have to keep plugging away. But he was pretty damn confident his DNA wasn't going to tell us anything incriminating. When I asked him for a swab, he didn't bat an eye."

I said, "That being the case, I suppose waiting six or seven weeks for results doesn't bother you very much."

"It is what it is, but I hate loose ends, and it's one that we need to tie up."

He opened his desk drawer and took out a tri-fold pamphlet. "Here, read this," he said, and handed it to me. "We might as well knock off for today. Maybe we'll hear from Dr. Markham pretty soon. I'll phone her in the morning and find out where she is with the facial reconstruction."

That evening, Diane grilled burgers and hot dogs on our patio while I read the key points on the status of DNA analysis in the tri-fold pamphlet that Vito had handed me. The FBI began its database eight years ago, in 1990, and Congress passed the DNA Identification Act in 1994. The system's official name is the Combined DNA Index System or CODIS. It is set up to encompass three indexes: the offender index, containing profiles of people convicted of crimes; the arrestee index, consisting of those arrested for crimes but not necessarily convicted; and the forensic index, consisting of profiles collected from crime scenes but not yet tagged to a suspect. Altogether, there were currently about seven million profiles in the system, and to date, CODIS has processed evidence from over two hundred thousand investigations and has produced thousands of hits.

The remaining two-thirds of the pamphlet was replete with technical jargon, graphs, and statistics that did not concern me at the moment, mostly because I didn't fully understand it, and it made my head swim. The bottom line for me was that we had gotten a saliva swab that might help catch a killer who had remained anonymous for almost fifty years -- if, and it was a big if, we could connect the swab's DNA to some stored evidence from the crime scene.

Trying not to think about it, I put the pamphlet aside, sipped winc, and listened to soft classical music from our Bose system on the patio with my wife.

We talked about my daughter's wedding, which was coming soon, just a few weeks away. Joy and her fiancé, Michael Bettinger, were both aspiring journalists. Well, he wasn't so much "aspiring" anymore because he had landed a job at the Pittsburgh Press, but he had to begin by doing light reporting on community events. He would have to work his way up to the opinion pieces and investigative reports he strongly desired to write. Joy was still working on her doctoral thesis and would soon wrap it up. By working side by side with me on some of my movies, she was leaning these days toward becoming a television reporter, not strictly a print journalist. I felt that she and her Michael were a great match, and I was thankful that it was one part of our lives that was turning out just fine. So far. One never knew what tragedies might be waiting in anybody's life. Like any parent, I never stopped worrying about Joy and hoping she would continue to enjoy the happiness she deserved. I wasn't a religious person, so I didn't pray about it unless fervent hopes were somehow the equivalent of prayers.

CHAPTER 31

The time-of-delivery estimate on the DNA report would put us into mid-April of 1998 before we could start anticipating it. But putting a face on the skull that Vito and I had found had been promised for roughly the first week of that month. We were stalled till then, so I worked some more on my book, *Dealey Plaza*, during the intervening four or five weeks.

When I first started the book in the mid-eighties, I planned to compose it in sections named for our presidents that would cover key events in the lives of the main characters in each time frame, down through the decades from the Kennedy Administration to the Reagan Administration. But by now, since I hadn't finished the book due to other obligations, history was still being made and moving inexorably well past where I had originally intended to take the book. If I wanted it to be timely, I had to make the characters "live" past Carter and Reagan and all the way through George H. W. Bush and Bill Clinton. Maybe even further than that if I couldn't wrap it up soon. It was hard for me to chop it off amid the history that was even now being made because I thought it was the most important book I had ever undertaken. The five main characters had started modestly in life. Still, by now, they had become iconic Americans, successful in various areas of endeavor and very much in the national spotlight. Lori McCoy, the central heroine, was now a country western star and a movie star; her ex-husband Keith was a wealthy health-food guru; her sister was a leading feminist and an officer of NOW; her latest husband was a New York agent, prominent in national politics; and Frank Williams, through whose eyes the story was mostly told, had started in life wanting to be a novelist, but the murder of three of his friends by neo-Nazis had caused him to join the FBI and eventually lead an anti-terrorist unit. I intended to let the story build to the point where all five major characters attend their college reunion, and a person connected to the long-ago original murders is up in a tower with a rifle, wanting to kill them all.

In late April, I was hard at work, taking the novel forward, when Dr. Markham phoned to tell me that her reconstruction of the skull's face was ready to be unveiled. I supposed that she meant this figuratively -- I didn't picture her whipping aside a curtain. Vito and I could barely control the excitement of anticipation, and we sped to the Pitt campus in my Lexus. She could see how antsy we were, so without any chit-chat, she led me and Vito into a workroom where she did her sculpting, and there it was, on a pedestal.

My mouth went dry, and I started sweating and trembling the way I used to do in my childhood nightmares. I almost wanted to back away and flee from the room.

The hair needed to be corrected. The eyes were the wrong color.

But it was Mr. Brevko, my seventh-grade English teacher.

Vito's stare pierced me. He could see how shaken up I was. He put his hand on my shoulder.

Dr. Markham looked scared and worried. She said, "What's the matter? Have I done something wrong?"

"I recognize him," I announced a bit shakily.

"Who?" Vito asked me.

"My English teacher from seventh grade. Mr. Brevko." I almost didn't believe those words were coming out of my mouth.

Vito took a step or two back from the likeness, then stepped around it from side to side, examining it closely. Finally, he murmured, "Harvey Brevko...I didn't work on his case; it was mostly the county vice squad. But I was there when he was jailed. He got out on bail, then he disappeared before his trial." He turned toward Dr. Markham. "Well, thanks to you, we have him back. Part of him anyway."

I had pulled myself together, and now I managed to say, "You did a marvelous job, and I thank you. You and Dr. Kessler."

"This opens up a whole new area of inquiry for our investigation," Vito said.

"I hope it's not more than you bargained for," Dr. Markham said. But I'm glad you're pleased with my work. I'd like to see some photos of Harvey Brevko so I can critique what I've done. It will help me see how close I've come."

"His mug shot will be in the old file," Vito told her. "And there may be other photos of him by himself, I'm not sure. Maybe we can request his college graduation composite. There are plenty of other kinds of photos in his file, I'm sure. He was arrested for corrupting children sexually. He took photos of them in the nude."

"My God! I had no idea what this would lead to," said Dr. Markham. "This bust will now belong to the police department. You paid for it. I've taken several photographs of it, and I'll give them to you to take with you."

"Yes, we'll need them," said Vito.

"You can have them, " she said.

He looked closely at me and said, "Are you okay?"

I nodded. But I needed to figure it out.

He scrutinized me even more closely with those deep, dark eyes of his. It was as if he suspected me of something he didn't want to say.

CHAPTER 32

Vito and I went to the Terrace Garden while memories of how much I had loved Mr. Brevko's English class and his ego-building pep talks tumbled through my mind, along with the shock and hurt I felt when he was arrested and charged as a pedophile. At the time, I was too young and inexperienced to deal with that disillusionment. But now I told Vito about it, sitting at a table by ourselves in the dining room, and vestiges of the sickening feelings that had hit me long ago hit me again. We talked in low voices even though no one was in the place but us because it was too early for the normal lunch hour.

After a while, Vito said, "Let's go into the dining room. There's nobody in there, not even a waitress. I've got to ask you something, and I don't want you to get mad."

I went with him with a strange feeling of trepidation. We took our beers with us and found a table for two in a far corner. He stared at me for a long while.

"What the hell is bugging you?" I was finally forced to ask.

He said, "I guess there's no tactful way of asking you, Dave. But I have to. Did you kill Harvey Brevko?"

I was stunned, flummoxed. But I saw that he was serious. "Fuck no!" I blurted. "I hope this is a fucking joke."

He took his time with another sip of beer, then leaned back. "Dave, I hope you can realize that I needed to ask that. You helped me find Brevko's remains. It was even your idea to go looking. If somebody is arrested and goes on trial, any defense attorney, even an incompetent one, is going to make hay out of that. He or she will use you to make up an alternate theory of his murder. You'll be accused even if you're never put on the stand. Your name will be dragged through the dirt, especially because of the kind of movies you make."

Aghast, I said, "But I was only twelve years old when the guy disappeared!"

Vito said, "I don't think that matters. These days, there are lots of true stories people watch about killer kids. And you had motive, by your admission. Brevko used to be one of your idols in junior high school, but he turned out to be a rat."

"Goddamn it, Vito! I didn't *kill* him! You're an asshole for bringing it up."

"You're reacting exactly the way I didn't want you to. And if a defense attorney gets you rattled this way, it's gonna make you look guilty."

I didn't say anything more right then. I just leaned further away from Vito and tried to see it his way.

"Think about it," he pressed. "I don't think you killed him; I'm just trying to prepare you for what might happen. Let's just hope we find the killer and nail him in such a way that there isn't any reasonable doubt."

I worked hard to see it his way and told myself I didn't want to lose his friendship. He let me be for a long while. Then he reached out his hand, and I shook it.

I grimaced, then forced a slight, despairing smile.

Vito said, "We've got to track down Brevko's wife. If we can find her, it's a good place to start. We must see if we can dig up his old dental records to confirm that it's him. The wife might know where they might be. We have to find out who killed him. It might have something to do with the deaths of the three boys."

"Too coincidental not to," I ventured.

The tension between Vito and me was mainly gone now.

The waitress came to us, and we ordered fish and fries.

"Let's each have a shot and a beer," Vito said. "I'll buy."

I nodded, and the waitress wrote our order into her pad.

As she walked away, Vito said, "I can see several scenarios at work here. One, Brevko's murder and the murders of the boys are totally unrelated, even though it's a possibility. Two, Brevko's wife killed him in a fit of rage after finding out what he was arrested for. Three, he killed the boys, and somebody knew it and killed him."

"Or, four," I said, "somebody killed him in those woods, and one or all three of the boys witnessed it, so he or she had to eliminate them."

"It couldn't be she," Vito said, "because of the semen in Joey's underpants."

"Unless it's his semen," I said. "We don't know what he was doing before he was tied up. Maybe he was masturbating."

Vito thought about that and grimaced distastefully. "We'd be hard-pressed to match.

Joey's DNA to the semen, even if we exhumed the body. He was embalmed, and we know that formaldehyde destroys DNA. So, an exhumation would be futile, even if Pamela or Armand Angelo would consent to it."

"This is maybe a wild thought after all these years," I said. "But she might have an old hairbrush that has strands of the boy's hair in it. Or she might have taken a lock of his hair before he was buried, like some people do. Back in the day, people kept loved ones' hair in lockets or pressed it between bible pages. I find it morbid, but that's me."

"Me, too, that's for sure," said Vito. "After we eat, let's head back to my office. We can search for Harvey Brevko's wife. If I can't turn up anything useful, I'll get a detective at the police department to do it. They have access to files that I don't."

***

I remembered that my father had told me when I was twelve that Mr. Brevko's wife was divorcing him and moving "far away from here" after he was arrested. The issue on that was, had she gotten the divorce papers filed before he was killed or not? And even if she had brought them filed, but the divorce had not gone through yet -- which it couldn't have -- were they still legally considered man and wife to this very day?

Perhaps she had moved to another town and filed the divorce papers there. Or maybe she hadn't filed them after he could no longer be found to be served. Perhaps she had known he was dead, even if she hadn't killed him. Maybe someone else had done it for her.

Vito and I discussed all these possibilities while we drove to the Clairton Municipal Building, where the police department, the mayor's office, and all other municipal bureaus and agencies were installed. He wanted to pull the old file on Harvey Brevko so he could go through it for information that had been gathered on Brevko's wife when he was arrested in 1951. Lucky for us, it was still an open file because he had disappeared before there could be any resolution to his case. Vito explained to me that back then, it was hoped he would eventually be apprehended and the trial would go forward. We took the file, in a tattered brown accordion-style legal folder, back to the conference room in his office building. He started going through it while I opened my laptop and, in lieu of anything else to do, tried to turn up scraps of info on my own.

"Her name was Alicia," Vito told me. "Alicia Brevko. Twenty years old back then. I was quite taken with her. A looker. A sexy way about her, too."

Of course, those attributes were the first ones that I would have expected Vito to notice in a woman. "How the hell did she get hooked up with a deviate like Harvey Brevko?" he added.

"Beats me," I said because I couldn't think of what else to say.

As he continued to pull out and thumb through the manila folders in the accordion-type file, he wrote things down and passed along the essential facts that he uncovered to me.

We learned that Alicia Brevko left Harvey only a few days after he was arrested and charged. She told the vice detective that she had to get their one-year-old daughter, Sarah, away from him in case he got out on bail, which he did. She also said that she was going to file for divorce because she was scared that if she didn't, baby Sarah might be taken away from her by Child Protective Services. Meanwhile, the file showed that Alicia had temporarily moved in with her parents on Wiley Avenue in Clairton while she started trying to get her life back in order. The parents' names were in the file, and so was their address, and their last name was Nevins.

"See what you can find on them," Vito said. "Andrew and Josephine Nevins."

That was easy enough. I searched out their obituaries. Both were deceased in the 1980s, and a couple unrelated to them was now living in their house on Wiley.

After Vito gleaned all the useful information he could from the old file, he computer-searched the Pennsylvania Department of Vital Records for both Alicia Brevko and Alicia Nevins in case she had reclaimed her maiden name out of embarrassment. That was the case, at least for several years, until she remarried and became Alicia Moore. Utilizing that discovery, he Googled the Pennsylvania Department of Transportation website, the same site that traffic-control cops searched when they stopped someone for a driving violation or accident and discovered that Alicia Moore still had a license in this state.

He pulled up her license photo, printed it, and showed it to me. She was now 66 and living in Harrisburg, Pennsylvania, the state capital. She was still attractive for her age, with a pleasant smile and silvery hair trimmed short and neatly parted. Working from her driver's license address, Vito found that she had a listed phone number. He and I both wrote it down.

We spent some additional time looking up and taking notes on Alicia's path through life after fleeing her first husband. We discovered that her second husband, Donald Moore, was a retired schoolteacher. Digging further, I found an article in the *Harrisburg Leader-Democrat* about Mr. Moore being chosen Teacher of the Year in 1992. There was a photo of him smiling and holding a framed certificate.

"What does it say he taught?" Vito asked me.

"High school English."

"I'll be damned, she married an English teacher," Vito said. "Same as her first husband. I hope he doesn't have any of the same predilections."

I said, "Maybe that was her goal. To set things right by marrying a guy like Harvey in every way except one."

"That's too heavy for me," Vito said.

"What do we do next?" I asked him.

"There's no use sitting around with our thumbs up our butts. I'm gonna try Alicia's phone number right now, see if I can catch her at home."

He was successful. Once again, he put me on speakerphone to hear how she responded to his revelations. After some preliminary chit-chat designed to help

Alicia recovered from the shock of hearing from a detective at this late date. He said to her, "I'm sorry to tell you this, but we have some news about your ex-husband, Harvey Brevko, and I'm afraid it's not good. We need to talk with you in person. We can drive to Harrisburg tomorrow if that suits you."

"But I haven't seen or heard from him for years and years," she protested. "I don't know a thing about where he's been or what he's been doing."

I was pretty sure that Vito wasn't going to dump on her that Harvey had been slowly decaying in a makeshift grave, and he didn't. Instead, he said, "Some things have come up that make it necessary for me to find out all I can about how things were between the two of you when he got arrested. After you and I talk, I'll be able to tell you a lot more about the present situation."

"Well...all right," she said reluctantly. "I'll still be home tomorrow, but my husband and I are going to leave the day after that to visit my daughter and our grandchildren."

"If we leave Pittsburgh very early in the morning, we should be at your house by ten A.M. Is that okay?"

Once again, she hesitated but then agreed.

"Progress!" Vito said. "There's nothing like it! It's been a long day, Dave. Let's go home and get plenty of rest."

As I gathered my things he gave me another hard look and said, "Are we still buddies?"

I said, "Damn right," and shook his hand.

CHAPTER 33

Harrisburg is 180 miles from Pittsburgh on the Pennsylvania Turnpike, approximately a three-and-a-half-hour drive from when Vito and I got on the Pike at Irwin, PA, and kept going without stopping. We drove it in my Buick after having breakfast at a Bob Evans in Irwin, off Route 30.

We were both excited about talking with Alicia Moore because we had a feeling that the case was at long last heating up and maybe on the verge of that much maligned and inaccurate word, closure. It had haunted my life for almost half a century. As William Faulkner once said, the past is not only not dead, but not even past. As an English major with a history minor, I've always had a feeling for the continuity of time, and I've cultivated it. Many things people considered "ancient history" didn't seem so long ago. Sometimes, I would point out to them and remind myself that two thousand years ago, when Jesus lived, it was only twenty long lifetimes ago. My father, born in 1906, was four years old when Mark Twain died. Mark was 25 at the start of the Civil War in 1860, and Jesse James was about seventeen. If Jesse hadn't been assassinated and had done some prison time and then lived to a ripe old age, he'd have been in his fifties when my grandfather came here from Italy during the Spanish-American War. Pancho Villa was still galloping and gunning down gringos in 1926. Butch Cassidy's family maintained that he was not killed in Bolivia but returned to the U.S. and died of cancer in 1937, two years before I was born and World War Two broke out.

There is an inevitable continuity to history, an intertwining of events, that most people are oblivious to.

Now Vito and I were on the verge of connecting one murder that had gone undiscovered till recently with three murders that had been long known about and had affected us personally. Our newest step in that direction was our trip today to Harrisburg to talk with Alicia Moore, the wife of one of those murder victims.

She and her second husband, Donald, lived in a modest brick ranch on a side street near the capitol and the legal district. They were both home, let us in as soon as we rang the bell, and offered us coffee, which we accepted. They were both wearing their stay-at-home clothes: he was in a T-shirt and jeans, and she was in a plaid blouse and jeans, but he had shaved and put on lipstick. The four of us sat around the dining table in a living room, a dining room combination with good furniture and cheerful accouterments. Donald and Alicia came across as a pleasant middle-aged couple who had probably led lives guarded from unusual tragedies. In other words, not like the life Alicia had led with Harvey Brevko, which had ended with perverse criminality.

Vito didn't tell her right away that her first husband was dead and had been for a long time. He wanted to feel her out first. After all, there was some chance that she already knew he was long gone if she had killed him or paid to have it done.

After we got down to business, his first question was, "When Harvey skipped out on his sentencing hearing, where did you think he went?"

She answered immediately, "My first thought was to phone his parents. They lived in Trenton, New Jersey. Frankly, they always enabled him and thought he could do no wrong. They would let him get away with anything from childhood on. When I married him, I had no idea how pampered he was. He expected me to continue pampering and enabling him."

"Your marriage was a one-sided thing?"

Alicia said, "That would be an understatement."

"Did you ever suspect that he was doing anything, shall we say 'wrong,' with his cameras and his picture taking?"

She thought about that, then said, "No, maybe I should have, but I didn't. I was glad that he was such a well-liked teacher. When he got permission from the school to start his so-called photography club, ten or twelve students immediately signed up. And they were wildly enthusiastic -- I saw that when I popped in on one of the after-school meetings. He even got the school board to authorize an expenditure of two hundred dollars for several cheap cameras and lighting equipment for the kids to take turns signing out."

Vito said, "He wasn't still holding photography club meetings at the time of his arrest. How did that come about? Were you aware of it?"

"Yes, I was," Alicia answered.

For my part, I keenly recalled that I would have been in sixth grade, still at Miller Avenue School, when Mr. Brevko's photography club was discontinued. I had heard about it when I began seventh grade and was sorry that it didn't still exist because I naively wanted more exposure to my favorite teacher.

Alicia said, "He told me that too many of the kids had lost interest, so it was down to only two or three members. He said it had been fun while it lasted, a statement that later made me shudder every time I thought of it."

"Was there any length of time when you believed his explanation?"

"Yes, I never thought much about it till he was arrested. He tried to set me up for the fact that his arrest was going to occur. He said that some of the boys in the club had taken some nasty photos of some of the little girls, and the police were accusing him of turning a blind eye and letting it happen."

"That must have been around when I already had him under investigation," Vito said. "He knew the ax was about to fall."

"And then you came to our house," Alicia said grimly. "I was there with Sarah; in fact, I was feeding her baby food. I remember it was carrots – awful-looking stuff, but she liked it. I hurried up and wiped her mouth with her bib, and went to the door. And there you were. I was startled. I didn't know what to expect. You didn't beat around the bush. You asked if you could come in, and then you told me Harvey was arrested."

"You didn't beat around the bush either," said Vito. "You told me that Harvey had already made you aware that some of the boys in the photography club had taken nasty pictures. So, if that was why I was there, he wasn't to blame."

"I was trying hard to still believe in him. You asked if we could sit down and talk, so I led you into the kitchen, and you questioned me while I finished feeding Sarah."

Vito had told me all this as we drove across the Pennsylvania Turnpike, but now I was hearing it recounted by both the detective and the subject, so I was intently following all of it. And so was Alicia's current husband, Donald Moore. Of course, I was taking notes, and he wasn't.

Alicia finally asked, "So, why are you here today, after all this time, Detective Martinelli? You wouldn't be wasting your time unless it's something very important."

"We'll get to that," he hedged. "First I want to thoroughly cover old ground, so we're on the same page going forward. You said that when Harvey disappeared and we couldn't find him, the first people you thought of where his parents."

"But they were stunned and said he wasn't there. And I believed them. Apparently, so did you when you came back asking more questions."

"You told me you had been preparing to take Sarah and move out of the house, but now you decided to stay a while longer, now that Harvey had run off."

I knew this because Vito had already told me, during our drive over here, that when Alicia told him she was staying for a while, it made him look even harder at her as a suspect in Harvey's disappearance. Why would she not get out of town right away unless she knew he was dead and never coming back? And the same possibility had gotten new life now that we had identified his skull.

"Where do you think Harvey might be nowadays?" Vito asked.

Alicia said, "I assure you, I have no idea. I don't know and don't care. I had to wait seven years to petition a court to have him declared legally dead, so I could collect on his meager life insurance and put the money aside for Sarah's education. Also, so I could marry Donald. It wasn't easy persuading the judge. But finally, I got it accomplished."

"How did the two of you meet?" Vito asked. "How long have you known each other?"

"We met at a Christmas party for the high school faculty at the American Legion about a year before Harvey got arrested. We barely knew each other for a long time after that. We had met, but that's all. We weren't carrying on an affair, if that's what you're asking."

Vito mulled that over, then said, "I asked you this way back, but now I'm going to ask it again. Can you think of any enemies that would have wished harm on your first husband?"

"Before his arrest, I could have thought of nobody like that. But afterward, there were plenty of parents who hated him. Before I sold the house and got out of there, I had to change the listed number on the landline. I was getting too many threatening phone calls."

"Was there anybody you were terrified of?"

"Mostly, they would try to disguise their voices. I didn't know any of them very well anyway. In any case, there was no one I could point a finger at, or I would have filed for a restraining order."

"Nobody who would have wanted Harvey dead?" Vito said more succinctly.

Donald broke into the conversation for the first time. "Oh-oh, are you telling us something?"

He and Alicia were now on alert, waiting for a shoe to drop.

Vito said, "Harvey Brevko is dead and has been for all these years. His remains have been found in the woods in Clairton. That's why I'm here. Somebody killed him back then, and it's my job to make sure they don't get away with it for much longer."

Donald Moore said, "What about the boys and girls Brevko victimized? Wouldn't their relatives and friends be suspects? Because of the possible revenge motive?"

"That's a whole other can of worms," Vito said, "because the names of the abused kids weren't made public, and their involvement in the case was expunged after the case went totally cold. Keeping the kids safe from embarrassment that might have damaged them emotionally even more than they were already the main objective. That's why Harvey was offered a plea deal -- so none of the kids would have to testify at a trial."

"In other words," Mr. Moore said, picking up on Vito's point, "it would be tough, if not impossible at this late date, to track down the kids who were abused."

"Not only that," said Vito, "even if we knew who they were, none of them might also want to talk. The whole thing is a part of their past they probably don't want to be dug up. And who could blame them?"

***

191

During our drive back from Harrisburg, Vito and I ascertained that we both pretty much believed that Alicia Moore hadn't killed anybody. However, we still had to keep the possibility open. We figured that our more likely suspects probably belonged to the overwhelmingly massive pool of parents, relatives, friends, or just plain irate citizens who, out of anger over what Harvey Brevko had done to some of the kids in his photography club, had chosen to kill him.

We continued to postulate that perhaps one or all three of the boys found dead in the pond had either witnessed or somehow gotten wise to whoever had killed Brevko and had been murdered to shut them up.

The kicker was the semen in the underpants and the DNA report that hadn't come in yet.

If the semen belonged to the killer, it could be somebody who sodomized Joey and was seen doing it by the two other boys, and therefore he had to kill all three.

We realized that we would have to comb the Murder Book for leads toward the murdered boys' families and friends and make a list of them. We decided we should first write down all the mothers' and fathers' names, then go on from there to include siblings, aunts, and uncles. After that, we could potentially widen the list to include close family, friends, and others. This was a daunting task. We hoped that, somehow, we'd get to the point where we could focus more sharply on a specific person of interest. But it might take us weeks, if not months, to complete all the interrogations.

As we exited the Pennsylvania Turnpike and were still more than a half hour from Clairton, where I would drop Vito off, we decided not to begin that looming mountain of painstaking work until tomorrow. We had done plenty for today and couldn't face doing anymore.

I said, "Man, this is going to be a long, long list of suspects. I think we should divide it into two main subdivisions: those who are still alive and those who aren't."

"I'm hoping the killer is still living," Vito said. "Because if he's dead, we can't talk to him, threaten him, or flush him out. The case will go totally cold again, possibly forever."

His cell phone buzzed, and he fished it out of his breast pocket, flipped it open, and said, "Martinelli."

The voice on the other end of the line was so loud I could tell it was Pamela Angelo. "I need to see you!" she shrieked. "He hit me with his cane! He almost knocked me out! I thought he was going to kill me!"

"Who? Armand?"

"No! Santa Claus!"

Taking that sarcasm in stride, he said, "I'm not in Clairton right now, but I'm on my way there, Pamela. Can it wait till tomorrow?"

"I want to file a restraining order before the sonofabitch kills me, or I kill him first."

"What in the world set him off?"

"I told him you were asking about Joey's knife. And I told him that I know where it is!"

Vito and I both perked up and eyed each other like maybe we were going to get lucky.

He said, "Go to my office building, Pamela. One of the lawyers or their secretary will let you in. Wait for me and Aaron Cristi. We'll get there as fast as we can."

"Please hurry! I'm not making this up!"

"I believe you. But how do you know where Joey's knife is after all these years?"

"Because I put it there. I didn't want to tell you; I thought I'd get arrested for hiding evidence."

"So, where is it, Pamela? Don't worry, I'm not going to arrest you."

"It's in Joey's coffin. I told you; he loved that knife. I made sure it was buried with him so he could have it with him in heaven."

"Why didn't you turn it over to me then?"

"I didn't find it under Armand's old, ragged underpants in his dresser till after Biff and they were sentenced. I thought, like everybody else, that they were the killers -- so the knife didn't matter anymore, and Armand didn't do anything wrong.

CHAPTER 34

Pamela Angelo was waiting for us at Vito's office when we arrived from Harrisburg. She jumped up from her chair in the waiting room as soon as she saw us. She said, "I got two suitcases packed and in my car trunk. No way am I gonna go back to my house!"

Who could blame her? She had a black eye, a cut across her right cheek, and a bloody, half-clotted laceration of her scalp, which she bent over to show us by pulling her thinning gray hair aside.

"Where will you go?" Vito asked. "Do you have a safe place?"

"With my sister, Ellie. Her husband died, and she has a spare room. He treated her well, but the good died young. Why didn't God take mine?"

Vito and I ushered her into the conference and calmed her down. He brought her a soft drink and a package of cheese crackers. She munched on them while he questioned her to reconstruct what she had already told him on his cell phone while we were on the Turnpike, about how she had recovered the knife and what she had done with it. Vito recorded everything she had to say, and I took copious notes for backup.

It was very late and very dark out by the time I pulled into my own garage. Diane and I kissed and hugged, and I told her there had been some significant developments. She fixed me a grilled cheese, tomato soup, and hot chocolate, and I felt human again. After I ate, I just bottomed out in front of the TV, in my recliner, while the TV show Diane was watching blurred past my eyes, unseen. She could tell I was still trying to cope with the day's events, so she left me to my thoughts. But that night, lying in bed, I confided in her and brought her up to speed on where Vito and I now were on the two separate, but almost certainly connected, murder cases.

We talked it over briefly, and I answered all her questions. After that, she fell asleep quite easily, even when stressful things were happening, but I tossed and turned fitfully through most of the night.

The following morning, I was half slumped at the kitchen table while she toasted bagels for each of us and brewed a pot of coffee.

She turned from the toaster and said, "You and Vito might be able to save yourselves a lot of work if you find a way of shaking up Armand Angelo. If he's the killer, and you can make him confess, it's game over, right?"

"Well, that's certainly true. But he's a feisty old fart, even though he's in failing health. I'm glad his wife is out of there. If we have any chance of nailing him, she will be a vital witness."

Setting a bagel and a pot of cream cheese in front of me, she said, "You told me it'd be futile to have Joey's body exhumed because DNA is destroyed by embalming fluid."

"Yes, according to what Vito said and my research."

"But Armand Angelo probably doesn't know that," Diane said.

"It may be somewhat of a moot point," I told her. "As Joey's biological mother, Pamela's DNA would be a pretty close match to his; they would share at least half of the markers, which would have a good chance of standing up in court. She also said that she does have a few strands of her son's hair in a little ring box in her jewelry case. She didn't bring it, but we can probably get a search warrant. If any of the hairs have roots, DNA might be able to be extracted."

"None of this sounds like a slam dunk," Diane said.

I showered and dressed and drove to Vito's office, where we were going to try to devise a precise plan for the future.

"Does it bother you," I asked him, "that we're trying to set a trap for an eighty-year-old man with an amputated leg and a colostomy bag?"

"Not for a New York minute," he said. "Or even a New York second. What bothers *me* is that he probably killed four people. His guilty conscience has probably been eating him up inside and contributed to his health problems. Which he richly deserves."

I said, "Pamela has got to sign off on the exhumation order. Doesn't she?"

"Not if we can get a judge to do it on the premise that it will help solve a multiple-murder case. We'll have to present an argument that Joey's DNA is needed to convict a murderer. And state in our affidavits that there's a high probability that either Joey's blood or the killer's blood is on the knife that his mother placed in his coffin. One of the lawyers in my office building can draw up the papers and help us get them to the right judge."

"What can we do in the meantime?" I asked. "Do we have to just sit on our hands till the exhumation is scheduled?"

"I'd like to find out everything we can about Armand Angelo," Vito said. "We know a lot about his doings from the day Joey went missing, but we don't know what was going on in his life before that, in other words, prior to his marriage and his becoming the boy's stepfather. Maybe there's violence in his past, for all we know, even though he doesn't have a rap sheet. If nobody ever pressed charges against him, stuff like that can fly below the radar."

"How are we going to find out? Talk to his old friends and acquaintances? Maybe his family members, if any of them are still alive?"

"That would be a way to start," said Vito. "Pamela should be able to point us in the right direction."

CHAPTER 35

It turned out that Pamela Angelo would only point us in a different direction.

She was killed at her sister's house three days after she moved in. Her sister, Ellie Johnson, found her mutilated body and totally freaked out. She revealed that she tried to dial 9-1-1 and got it wrong several times before finally getting through to the operator.

The way Pamela was mutilated was kept under wraps by the Clairton Police Department, but Vito leveled with me about it, and it was one of the most brutal blows I've ever had to take. I'm still not over it, even as I write about it twenty years later. The crime scene photos are burned into my brain.

Pamela was sprawled in a ghastly pool of dried blood in her sister's spare bedroom. There were shoe prints or boot prints tracked through the blood. There was blood spatter all over the walls, the bed, the drapes, and the rest of the furniture. Looking at all that made me squirm and avert my eyes. But then I was hit with the shock that topped all shocks --

Both her *ears* had been *sliced off!* It was the same thing that my fictional killer, Wayne Calley, did to each of his victims. He slit their throats and cut their ears off. But he took them with him for his necklace. This killer had left both of Pamela's ears on her bed.

For my entire career, ever since I made the first *Intensive Scare* movie, I had battled with censors and talking heads who castigated me for making "slasher movies." They accused me of inciting the worst impulses of my young fans, warping their minds and turning them into serial killers and mass murderers. In my worst, most soul-searching moments, I wondered if they might be right.

I knew that if Vito and I managed to solve Pamela's murder, the fact that she had been killed by the same M.O. used by a character that I had created would cause me to be vilified and despised. Nobody would care that I was trying to get at the roots of America's epidemic of mass violence in my most profound novel, *Dealey Plaza*. I would be dismissed as a shyster, a hypocrite, an enabler. Diane tried to console me and tell me that the worst I could imagine probably would not happen, but I didn't think she was right.

Since Vito was a special hire of the Clairton Police Department, he was now part of the team investigating Pamela Angelo's murder. And I was an adjunct or, as the chief put it, a "consultant." We briefed all the proper authorities, including two investigators from the Allegheny County Sheriff's Department who were also part of the team, on everything we had learned on our cold cases, which now seemed indisputably connected to what had been done to Pamela. Somebody clearly wanted me to mock me, or perhaps that unknown somebody was a sick fan of mine and believed he was paying me an "homage."

It didn't seem likely that a man with an amputated leg and a colostomy bag could have done everything that this delusional "Wayne Calley" had done to his victim. But Armand Angelo or somebody else could have enlisted him. Without Pamela to put on the witness stand, no evidence or hearsay testimony about Joey's knife would stand up in court. That was clearly the overriding motive for taking her out of the picture.

If the killer thought that killing her would stop the exhumation, he was wrong. The fact that she had been murdered made it even easier for the judge to grant our petition for Joey's body to be exhumed. It was given an imminent date on which it would take place: April 18, 1998, only a half week from now.

"Do we have to just sit on our hands till then?" I asked Vito.

"No, not at all. Let's follow through on our plan to learn as much as we can about Mr. Angelo's earlier life. That's even more important now than it used to seem.

Together, we pounded the pavement and put a lot of miles on my car over the next five days. We ferreted out anybody and everybody we could find who could potentially give us more information on Armand Angelo's past. Much of what we persisted in was fruitless and boring, but we gleaned a smattering of facts.

Armand Angelo, born in Clairton in 1927, fathered an illegitimate daughter, Patricia, in 1944, when he was only seventeen. He didn't give Patricia his last name; he didn't acknowledge his paternity or pay child support. But he lucked out because Patricia's mom, who was only 15 when she gave birth, within a year was wed to a boy aged eighteen, who was already working in a steel mill and making good money. This boy, Kevin Mackey, willingly adopted Patricia and gave her a decent upbringing. She graduated high school and went to work as a bank teller.

Patricia got married to a man named Alex Blanton, and they had a son named Steven in 1970. Thus, since Patricia was Armand Angelo's illegitimate daughter, Steven was not only Alex Blanton's biological son but also Armand Angelo's "illegitimate" grandson. He had never been acknowledged as such by anybody, especially Armand. Alex Blanton was a drunkard, a drug addict, and an abuser, and Patricia and Steven lived a miserable life with him, and the boy grew up in constant fear and poverty.

Steven obsessed over and despised the fact that when Armand Angelo was in his twenties and could have accepted his obligation to marry Steven's biological mother, he instead married Pamela and adopted *her* son, Joey.

According to some of the folks that Vito and I interviewed, Armand Angelo's unclaimed grandson, Steven, rabidly hated Joey and Pamela because, in his view, they had usurped positions in life that should have belonged to him and his mother, who died of pneumonia at a young age in a bitterly cold winter when her poor excuse for a husband, Alex Blanton, had, as usual, spent his pay on booze and drugs and did not buy coal for their antiquated coal furnace. Thus, the house was cold, which caused pneumonia.

Well, once Vito and I had learned all this, we had to inevitably consider Steven Blanton, who believed he should have been an Angelo, a possible suspect for Pamela Angelo's murder.

Meanwhile, the exhumation of Joey's remains was expected to proceed on schedule. That grisly event was to be counteracted by one of happiness and expectation—Diane and I were looking forward to my daughter's wedding. The rehearsal was to occur on the Saturday before the Tuesday when the coffin would be excavated.

I was a nervous wreck every time I thought about the upcoming wedding rehearsal because the announcement had been in the newspapers, and there had been one more ugly detail about Pamela Angelo's murder that had been withheld:

On one of the white walls of the bedroom, there was a message scrawled in her blood:

DAVID CRISTI!
ALL JOY WILL SOON END!
BEWARE! BEWARE!
YOUR BASTARD SON
WAYNE CALLEY

CHAPTER 36

In one of the terrifying scenes in *Intensive Scare*, Wayne Calley jimmies open a sliding glass door and creeps into a shadowy, dimly lit family room. He's wearing black gloves and a black ski mask. He's carrying a sharp bayonet and wearing his necklace of human ears.

The back story I gave him was that he was born to wealthy, outwardly sophisticated, but jaded parents who paid little attention to him while foisting him upon nannies and boarding schools. At age fourteen, he was kidnapped, and the kidnappers cut off his left ear and mailed it to his mother and father with a note telling them that their son's other ear would be cut off if they didn't pay a two-million-dollar ransom. They were slow paying, and he almost lost the other ear.

He killed his mother when he was fifteen years old and was sent to an institution for juveniles, where he was confined until he reached age eighteen. When he got out, he began raping and killing beautiful young women, then cutting off their ears, as renegade soldiers had done during the Vietnamese War.

By the time this particularly scary scene took place in my movie, the audience already knew the back story, and many of them were already shuddering, gasping, and holding their breath.

Wayne Calley crept from room to room, satisfying himself that no one was home. Then, in a sudden blind rage, he began trashing the family room. He yanked photos and mementos from the shelves and walls and stomped ceramic figurines and glass picture frames to bits, grinding them into the carpet. He snatched a cheerleading trophy from the fireplace mantel and hurled it against the bricks with a loud shatter.

He leaned against a wall, panting, but a tiny intrusive sound startled him. It was the scraping of a key being inserted into the front door.

A beautiful young woman in a smartly tailored gray pantsuit came into the living room, humming. Laden with department store packages, she deposited them on a table in the dining room, then walked down a hallway and into her bedroom, where she put her purse on her dresser.

She kicked off her high-heeled shoes and took off her clothes, stripping down to bra and panties. She examined her reflection in a full-length mirror, turning this way and that, assessing her lovely face and body.

Suddenly, Wayne Calley leaped at her from off-camera!

She shrieked and tried to fight back, clawing at him. But he overpowered her, held his bayonet to her face, and forced her down onto her bed. He got on top of her, his leather-jacketed arm pressing into her throat, his blade pricking her face, drawing a trickle of blood. He choked her so she couldn't cry out anymore.

Her eyes bulged as tears ran down her cheeks.

She whimpered beneath him, wide-eyed in her helplessness. He made his power over her last for an excruciatingly long time, taking his time to enjoy himself thoroughly. She sank into a form of catatonia, totally under his control. His thrusts became faster and faster until he cried out from the sheer intensity. For several long seconds, he savored the diminishing spasms. Then he pulled his trousers up.

In a sudden frenzy, he lunged at her, ramming his blade into her throat.

Blood gushed as the knife hit bone -- and he jumped back.

She writhed and kicked, then emitted a final whimper, a final gurgle.

She was totally still, her eyes gazing sightlessly at the ceiling.

He tugged at one of her ears and started to cut it...

CHAPTER 37

Joy's apartment was a modern, reasonably priced townhouse ten miles from downtown Pittsburgh. I had bought it as an investment, or at least that's what I told her, so she wouldn't feel bad when I let her live there without paying rent.

On the night of her wedding rehearsal and the customary dinner afterward, she and Michael Bettinger arrived shortly after ten o'clock. He escorted her to her front door, and they talked for a while. Then, he kissed her goodnight and drove away.

Under the glow of the porch light, she put her key in the lock and went inside. She made sure to lock the front door. So as not to scare her out of her wits and ruin the happy anticipation of her wedding, I hadn't told her about the awful message scrawled in Pamela Angelo's blood at the scene of her murder. But I couldn't help impressing upon her, more than usual, how important it was always to be as careful as possible. I couched my comments in references to a recent spate of suburban break-ins till she finally scolded me mildly that I was an old fuddy-duddy, and she was perfectly capable of living alone and taking the necessary precautions.

A light dimly lit the backyard of her townhouse on the outer wall of the patio, and the light faded to darkness at the fringes of the grass, bordered by foliage and a waist-high chain-link fence.

That's where the intruder was lurking.

He watched various lights turned on and off in Joy's kitchen, then her living room, till finally, a light went on in what he figured was her bedroom. He smiled in anticipation, putting on his ski mask and wielding a sharp knife. He was wearing a necklace of fake amputated ears, sold online at websites hawking photos, posters, and souvenirs dedicated to a slate of horror films. He wished he had kept Pamela Angelo's ears instead of forgetting them in a rush of adrenaline and panic and absent-mindedly leaving them on her bed. There was no question that he wanted to continue being like Wayne Calley now that he had felt the thrill of it to the depths of his soul.

He waited for a long time for Joy's bedroom light to be turned off. He forced himself to be exceedingly patient, one of the lesser qualities he knew he would have to cultivate. He waited a long time in the dark after the light was turned off till he was ready to take a chance that Joy had fallen asleep. He thought about the message he had left in red on a white wall, ALL JOY WILL END, and he thought it was perfect. Thinking about it gave him a delicious feeling. It was difficult for him to control his lust. He had had no desire whatsoever to have sex with the old woman he so much hated, Pamela Angelo, but Joy Cristi totally excited him. She was vivacious and beautiful; he had never had a woman so fine.

He hid for a long moment behind some garbage cans, looked all around to make sure all was well, then eased himself over the short chain-link fence and crept across the yard and onto the patio.

He had scouted the townhouse two nights before. He had seen, to his satisfaction, that there were no two-by-twos in the interior runner of the sliding glass door, a precaution that many people might take to prevent the door from sliding open even if the lock was breached. After taking another look all around the place, he used the thick blade of his knife to jimmy the door.

He listened—no sound of stirring from inside the house.

He slid the door open as slowly and silently as possible and let himself into the living room. Then he paused to allow his quickened breaths to slow down.

He crept farther into the room, his eyes on the open bedroom door down the hall -- and he jumped at the sound of a harsh voice.

"All right, Buster! Drop the knife!"

The angry voice at first came from a dark corner, maybe even from behind that big chair. Then, he was blinded by a bright beam of light.

"*Drop* the knife, *motherfucker!*"

He didn't know what to do. He didn't want to be caught.

Without even thinking, he stepped toward the voice behind the bright light. There was a loud blast, and a slug hit him so hard that he was knocked backward against a wall, and he fell. As a result, he dropped his knife.

Vito hit a light switch, and the living room was now bathed in light from a chandelier. He turned his flashlight off. He stood over the ski-masked intruder, who had blood pouring from his shoulder.

Vito said, "Get to your feet, asshole! Hands behind your back!"

As he cuffed the intruder, Joy appeared from the hallway, her startled face a mask of wonderment and fear.

"It's all right, honey!" Vito called out to her. "You're safe!"

Then I entered through the sliding glass door, holding a snub-nosed .38. I had no license to carry it, but it was a real gun that I had used many times as a prop in my movies.

Now that the intruder was handcuffed, Vito pulled off his ski mask.

We weren't shocked when we saw who he was.

Steven Blanton. Armand Angelo's illegitimate grandson. A wiry wastrel with a bony face and a washed-out look in his dead gray eyes.

I was so shaky I thought my prop gun might go off. I pointed it away from Steven out of fear that I might shoot him "accidentally." It was what a side of me dearly wanted to do.

I put the gun down on the table and tightly hugged Joy, so glad she was alive and had a future ahead of her.

Vito and I had been staking out her apartment ever since Pamela Angelo's killer had left that message scrawled in blood. For five days, we had been watching the townhouse furtively from concealment, Vito in the woods just beyond the fence and me in my car, parked a short distance away in the front street.

In the original *Intensive Scare*, Simon Rocail's first victim was a young woman just returning home from her wedding rehearsal. And so tonight, on a plausible hunch, we had decided that Vito should hide inside Joy's apartment, and I would hide close to the backyard. It was only earlier today that we had alerted my daughter to what we had been doing and what we thought we should be doing now. She was brave enough to agree.

I had attended the wedding rehearsal and dinner but had left early to station myself back from the chain-link fence ahead of Joy and Michael's arrival. We did not tell Michael what was going to happen after he left. We didn't want to risk that he might object or, worse, give our plan away inadvertently or on purpose out of fear for his bride-to-be.

We had been lucky and smart, and it had all played out close to how we had hoped. Now that it was over, and we could begin to unwind and gather our wits about us, Vito called 9-1-1 to get a wagon to take Steven to the Clairton Police Station. He wanted to interrogate him there. Everything had started in Clairton way back in 1952, and it was where he wanted to finish it.

In shackles in the small, windowless interrogation room, it didn't take the would-be Wayne Calley very long to confess. It wasn't so much that he wanted to unburden himself but that he wanted to brag. He admitted that he killed Pamela Angelo because Armand had paid him to do it. "Only five thousand dollars," he said. "But I enjoyed doing it."

Armand had not paid Steven to kill anybody else. But Steven had discovered that he liked *being* Wayne Calley and doing Wayne's thing.

In enlisting him to kill Pamela Angelo, Armand Angelo had revealed to Steven his true motive for the murders of long ago, and it was not in the realm of anything Vito and I had conjectured.

Steven said, "My grandfather told me that Joey was one of the kids that that faggot English teacher, Harvey Brevko, took dirty pictures of. Some of the pictures were of Brevko playing with Joey's penis. He turned Joey into a faggot, and Armand was trying to beat it out of him because he couldn't stand his stepson being like that. He hated Brevko with a passion. So, he met the teacher in a bar, tricked him into getting into his car, and parked behind the little store by the peach orchard on Farnsworth Avenue. Brevko thought they were there for sex, but Armand strangled him and dragged his body down the path and buried him in the woods above the shack."

"Then the young boys were killed," Vito said. "Did one of them see Armand killing Harvey Brevko?"

"No, none of them were wise to that."

"Then why did Armand kill all three boys?"

"He was mad that day, stomping down the alley with a leather belt in his hand, yelling for Joey, and trying to find out where Joey had run away. He went down the path to where the shack was, and he heard noises. When he sneaked up on the shack, he saw Joey blowing one of the boys and the other one masturbating while he was watching. All three were naked. Armand flew into a rage and held a knife to them and tied them up with their shoelaces one by one, and they were so scared they let him do it. They were embarrassed about what they were caught doing, and Armand said they were shaking all over, scared he was going to turn them in to the police and the principal at their school. He sliced Joey up worse than the others, even his genitals. Then he killed them and dumped their bodies in the pond."

Vito and I were filled with revulsion, but we had to hold it in until we got Steven's details on tape.

I was squirming under the guilt that Pamela Angelo's death was a copycat murder, and the murderer being copied was a fictional one that I had created. And all the murders down through the years had been set in motion by homophobia. It was an affliction that our entire society was still trying to heal, even though strides had been made in recent decades. In the arts, people's sexual preferences were accepted placidly and were not an issue. As Elizabeth Taylor once said, "If you took all the homosexuals out of Hollywood, there wouldn't *be* a Hollywood."

The artists among us are ahead of the rest of society in terms of social and cultural mores. A friend of mine who is a jazz drummer once said to me, "There's no prejudice in jazz. You can either play or you can't."

My father was prejudiced against "differences," but I had grown away from it. I'm not perfect, but there are some things that I've managed to get right. Unlike Armand Angelo, I had no prejudice against anyone for whatever their sexual preferences might be. I might offer yet another quote, this one uttered by feminist Clare Booth Luce, who Ronald Reagan awarded the Presidential Medal of Freedom. When President Bill Clinton was being impeached for lying to Congress about a sexual encounter with an intern, Ms. Luce said, "We should not be surprised by anything we happen to learn about anyone's sex life."

Sexual experimentation by pre-adolescent boys is common, in fact, virtually universal.

212

The range of human sexuality is broad, much broader, far-ranging, and multi-layered than many people will acknowledge or admit. Same-sex experimentation at a young age has little to nothing to do with whether a boy will be homosexual when he becomes a mature adult.

In any case, my boyhood friend Ron Demick didn't deserve to die for it. Neither did Mickey or Joey. And I was gratified that, at long last, I had helped bring them justice, even though they were past any realization of it.

When Vito finished interrogating Steven, he was shoved into a cell. I went with Vito to Steven's shabby, smelly apartment to search it for incriminating evidence that might make the case against him even more potent. We had his key because all the stuff in his pockets had been taken from him.

I was leafing through some crumpled-up papers on a battered and grimy coffee table in Steven's living room when Vito called out from the kitchen.

"Hey, David! Come here and look."

He pointed at the refrigerator.

Fastened to the door with a couple of Wayne Calley souvenir magnets was the staged publicity photo of Wayne about to slit my throat with his bayonet. It was the one I had signed and handed to Armand Angelo after he told me it was for a friend. I wondered how much of a part it had played in turning Steven into a Wayne Calley wannabe. One thing he had in common with Wayne was that neither was a combat veteran. They didn't suffer from war wounds, mental or physical. They didn't have PTSD. They were both twisted freaks of nature and nurture. They raped and killed because they wanted to.

"We'll leave it right there and have CSI take photos of it," Vito said. "Let's get out of here."

We went to Armand Angelo's house to arrest him. When we mounted the front porch, we became aware of a foul smell coming from somewhere inside the house. We rang the bell, but we were waiting for someone to answer.

Vito kicked the door in. He drew his weapon, and we both entered.

Armand wasn't in the downstairs rooms or any of the bedrooms. He was in the basement, hanging from the I-beam. His face was purple, and his tongue was fat and swollen, lolling out of his mouth. His prosthetic leg was dangling but fastened in place. His colostomy bag must have emptied because the front of him was wet and dark, and the smell down here was overpowering.

I couldn't suppress a body-wracking shudder, thinking about the day when I was six years old, running down the cellar stairs, pulling clothesline out of my mother's hands, desperately trying to stop her from hanging herself.

Now, those nightmares would probably return.

CHAPTER 38

In the latter half of that year, I buried myself in finishing *Dealey Plaza.* It was therapy for me after all the years of hoping that the murders of my friends would someday be solved.

When I submitted the manuscript, my New York literary agent rejected it. He said my fans expected horror novels from me, not history and social commentary. In other words, he had me pigeonholed. I tried to convince him that it was my best novel and that he shouldn't be giving it short shrift, but he wouldn't listen.

I published the novel anyway, with a small Pittsburgh company called Burning Bulb Publishing. It didn't get wide distribution, but so it garnered over two dozen five-star reviews on Amazon and gave me a great deal of personal satisfaction. It should be made into a miniseries, but I wonder if that will ever happen.

I'm at work on an outline for yet another horror novel and a screenplay based on it.

It's not an *Intensive Scare* sequel.

For more information on John Russo,
his books, movies, and official merchandise,
please visit:

www.TheJohnRusso.com

ABOUT THE AUTHOR

With 40 books published internationally and 19 movies in worldwide distribution, John Russo has been called "a Living Legend." He began by co-authoring the screenplay for the horror classic, *Night of the Living Dead*, and went on to build an iconic decades-long career.

His books on the art and craft of movie making have become bibles of independent production and have won a national award for Superior Nonfiction. Quentin Tarantino and many other noted filmmakers have stated that Russo's books have helped them launch their careers.

John Russo wants people to know he's "just a nice guy who likes to scare people" -- and he's done it with novels and films such as *Return of the Living Dead*, *Midnight*, *The Majorettes*, *The Awakening*, *Heartstopper*, and *My Uncle John is a Zombie!*

He's had a long, rewarding career, and he shows no signs of slowing down. In 2024, Lionsgate acquired a Western written by him, *The Night They Came Home*, about the murder spree perpetrated by the Rufus Buck gang, who were all hanged in 1895.

Russo's popularity among genre fans remains at a high pitch. He appears at many movie conventions each year as a featured guest, and hundreds of attendees come to his tables or to the bar to share drinks, jokes, and serious conversation.

www.ingramcontent.com/pod-product-compliance
Lightning Source LLC
Chambersburg PA
CBHW060921250626
47159CB00008B/3101